i hate
everyone
but you

GABY DUNN & ALLISON RASKIN

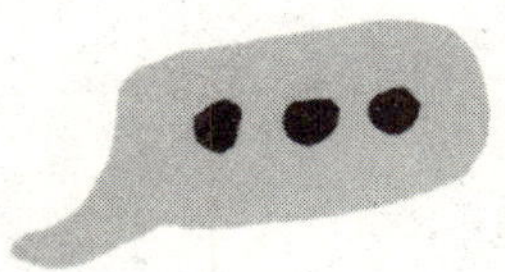

WEDNESDAY BOOKS
NEW YORK

This is a work of fiction. All of the characters, organizations, and events portrayed in this novel are either products of the authors' imaginations or are used fictitiously.

 For information, address St. Martin's Press, 175 Fifth Avenue, New York, N.Y. 10010.

www.stmartins.com

Designed by Anna Gorovoy

The Library of Congress Cataloging-in-Publication Data is available upon request.

ISBN 978-1-250-12932-1 (hardcover)
ISBN 978-1-250-12934-5 (ebook)



First Edition: September 2017

10 9 8 7 6 5 4 3 2 1

TO OUR PARENTS (OBVIOUSLY)

i hate
everyone
but you

## PLEASE CONFIRM RECEIPT OF THIS MESSAGE

**Ava Helmer** <AVA.HELMER@gmail.com>

to Gen

Dear Best Friend,

It is with a heavy heart that I write the first of what I can only imagine will be hundreds of emails detailing every second of our college-bound lives. I am extraordinarily proud of you and can't wait for the entire city of Boston to both love and fear you. Just remember that NO ONE will ever love (or fear) you like I do.

Grow! Flourish! Experiment with things so I don't have to. I will miss you every second of every day until you graduate a year early (hopefully) and return to me and the dry heat of the West Coast. Journalists can work anywhere, so don't try to pull "I need to move to New York" four years from now. You know I barely survived during your summer program in Temecula.

I can already tell that I will hate everyone but you.

Sincerely,

Ava Helmer
(that brunette who won't leave you alone)

P.S. My mother wants to make sure you bought a winter jacket. If not, she will ship you one using Amazon Prime.

**Re: PLEASE CONFIRM RECEIPT OF THIS MESSAGE**

---

**Gen Goldman** <GENX1999@gmail.com>
to Ava

We're still in the same room, you weirdo.

Stop crying.

G
(the blonde who is really uncomfortable with large displays of emotion)

**11:45 AM PST**

Are you at the airport?

Hello?

I hope you're at the airport because your flight takes off in 20 minutes.

Maybe your phone is dead. I hope your phone is dead and you are not dead.

**8:51 PM EST**

Landed.

Oh, thank God! I called your parents.

Sry. Phone died. Charged it. Fell asleep.

How was the flight? Do you want to come home?

Maybe in 4–6 months?? Hit on the steward & got some free peanuts.

Nuts are always free.

Depends on the kind . . .

Genevieve! Gross.

Did not blow the steward in the bathroom. If only for ur sake, my precious baby angel.

Plus he was gay.

I have to go pick out bedding with my mother. Call me when you get to your dorm.

I'll text u.

Get something stainproof.

Just saw that. GROSS!

## YOUR REPLACEMENT

---

**Gen Goldman** <GENX1999@gmail.com>
to Ava

Just kidding. Shannon could never replace you. Mostly because her parents must be mental to name her Shannon. How are the Helmers BTW? Do they miss their favorite should-have-been daughter? Your dad emailed me Boston tips from his one business trip five years ago . . . Apparently, the Marriott bar has KILLER chicken wings.

Still haven't heard from my parents. Hopefully they read my note. Can you be a runaway if you run away to a liberal arts college?

Back to my new BFF, Shannon. I hadn't even put my bag down before she stood up on her bed, popped open one of the ceiling tiles, and pulled out a bag of weed. I can already tell that she is going to be a lot of fun. But only when she's high.

Emerson isn't really a college campus so much as two buildings and a theater. Which is perfect, because I didn't even want to go to college. My RA says that the Boston Common (a big park) is our unofficial campus, but I've never seen a campus with so many meth heads.

I already love it here. I think I would blow my brains out if I was gated in somewhere with school spirit and a football team. It barely feels like school other than the optional classes. (JK. I know class is heavily encouraged.)

G

P.S. Don't be mad, but I took a Lyft to the airport. The driver was not a creep but he did hug me good-bye so it was basically the same as having a going-away party.

## Re: YOUR REPLACEMENT

**Ava Helmer** <AVA.HELMER@gmail.com>

to Gen

You took a Lyft to the airport?????

## Re: YOUR REPLACEMENT

**Ava Helmer** <AVA.HELMER@gmail.com>

to Gen

On second reading, the horrible saga of you going to the airport by yourself isn't even the worst part of that email. You can't let Shannon keep drugs in your room! Do you want to get expelled?? Because you will! I read the handbook for you.

I've been nervous reading all day. I now know far too much about how to properly brew tea from some weird booklet my mom refused to throw out. I move into the dorms tomorrow. Part of me wants to get there super early and sanitize the entire room and the other part of me doesn't want to go at all.

I know USC is only 13.1 miles from my house, but that's like an hour and a half in traffic.

Is it too late to get homeschooled? Or does that not work for higher education?

Just kidding. I'll be fine. Or I won't be fine and then I'll have to drop out and live in my parents' guesthouse until I sell my first script about living in my parents' guesthouse.

Thank God writers are meant to be crazy!

Ava

P.S. Flush the drugs. Seriously.

## Re: YOUR REPLACEMENT

---

**Gen Goldman** <GENX1999@gmail.com>
to Ava

You're not crazy. And I'm not flushing the drugs. They're not my drugs to flush. I already snorted, ate, and mainlined all of MY drugs. 😂😂😂

## Re: YOUR REPLACEMENT

---

**Ava Helmer** <AVA.HELMER@gmail.com>
to Gen

I can't believe my parents didn't trust you for two and a half years.

A

P.S. What do drugs taste like? Asking for a friend.

## Re: YOUR REPLACEMENT

---

**Gen Goldman** <GENX1999@gmail.com>

to Ava

Please refer to this video of Prince performing "Purple Rain":

http://bit.ly/purplerain

**7:14 PM PST**

I think my mom is crying.

U can just sense it? Like a bat signal?

My mom doesn't cry like a regular person. She just tightens up her face until the liquid squeezes out.

UR going to school 10 miles away

13.1.

You never listen to me.

**2:03 AM EST**

What was the picture you just sent? Have you been kidnapped by a blurry monster?

Girl who looks like you.

Why are you awake? It's 2 AM?

At a party. Gonna go kiss your twin to make sure it's not u.

It's not me! Cease and desist!

**2:11 AM EST**

Gen?

That was a quick spiral into meth.

**3:35 AM EST**

Meth tastes great! Going to bed! Xoxox

## I HAVE ARRIVED

---

**Ava Helmer** <AVA.HELMER@gmail.com>

to Gen

Do you remember the first day of freshman year (1.0) when I wore that weird sweater set and you spilled Diet Coke all over your white shirt, so I tried to give you my cardigan but you refused because only lame-ass bitches wear cardigans?

I wish that day was happening right now instead of this one.

My roommate, Jessica, is not very nice. And not in a I-have-a-rough-exterior-but-a-heart-of-gold Gen kind of way, but actually not nice. She asked me to take the left side of the room and then an hour later told me she wanted the left side. Which isn't a big deal EXCEPT I had already cleaned the left side and started organizing all my plastic drawers. (I wish you would get plastic drawers, they are a life changer.)

Jessica is a marketing major.

I feel like no other description is necessary.

USC feels even bigger than when I visited. The whole campus is packed with security guards, which somehow does the opposite of making me feel safe. I tried to find all my classrooms for Monday, but I ended up in four different dining halls instead.

Yes. There are four dining halls. And they all serve the same food.

Maybe I should go find Meghan. I know she is boring and dumb, but at least she is a familiar boring and dumb.

The one good thing about this place is everyone seems to party all the time, so it won't be hard to find out WHERE THE PARTY AT.

A

P.S. Are you dead?

11:16 PM EST

Abort Meghan. We just spent 4 years avoiding Meghan. Go meet new people.

You have great hair!

???

Just a confidence boost! 😎😺

## ADULTING

**Gen Goldman** <GENX1999@gmail.com>

to Ava

I was born to be an adult. Crushing this no-rules thing. Not that my house had many rules, but I felt like your mom was always watching. (What's up, Ruth! Are you still reading Ava's emails?!)

Anyway. Adult parties. I guess technically they are college parties, but more than five twenty-somethings made an appearance so I think it counts as a crossover.

Shannon took me to the baseball house in Allston, which I thought would be terrible but it's not even a real baseball team. It's just a bunch of guys who toss a ball around and make dinner together on Sundays. We stayed until 3 AM talking about *Stop Making Sense* and Spike Lee's MJ documentary (which is basically a fluff piece).

Shannon kind of sucks except as a conduit to fun. But I met this badass literature chick, Molly, who is basically me with shorter hair. We drank gin and tonics and laughed whenever boys would try to get us to “toss some balls around.” (Believe it or not, this pickup line ACTUALLY WORKED on Shannon.)

Brace yourself:

Molly is bisexual, but I guess almost everyone here is. She was wearing an unofficial Emerson T-shirt that said “Gay by May or Your Money Back.” I think she has a girlfriend. Or a boyfriend. “Charlie” could go either way. Just like everyone else at this school!

BOOM!

G

## Re: ADULTING

**Ava Helmer** <AVA.HELMER@gmail.com>
to Gen

That was a really great joke. Setup. Punch line. Are you sure you want to write actual news and not buddy comedies with me in Screenwriting 101?

For such a select group of young writers, most of the kids in my elite BFA program are fucking weirdos. We had an orientation, and half of my class said *The Shawshank Redemption* was their favorite movie. That can't be true, right? Some of those people probably haven't even seen that dreadful movie.

I couldn't pick between *Little Miss Sunshine* and *The Sapphires.* But no one had heard of *The Sapphires* so *LMS* won by default. I was worried about talking too much during the introductions so now I think I talked too little. People would just think I'm shy if I didn't have such harsh features that make me look like a bitch.

Am I a bitch? Does being judgmental automatically make you a bitch?

Looking forward to your thoughts and notes.

A

P.S. You went to a BASEBALL party? Who are you anymore?

**Re: ADULTING**

---

**Gen Goldman** <GENX1999@gmail.com>

to Ava

You are NOT a bitch. You just have taste. And high cheekbones.

Please refer to the baddest bitch in the game for assurance: NICKI MINAJ DEFENDS HER PERSONALITY & DENIES BEING A BITCH!

## Re: ADULTING

---

**Ava Helmer** <AVA.HELMER@gmail.com>

to Gen

Oh, Nicki Minaj. Once again reminding us what it means to be a boss.

**9:42 AM PST**

Sitting in my first official college class.

I'm the only one here.

Do you think I'm in the wrong place?

How early are u?

Only 15 minutes!

18 minutes!

UR in the right place. UR just a nerd.

Does no one else have panic attacks that they're going to arrive late and ruin their lives so they overcompensate by arriving extremely early?

I'm sure someone else does. And ull prob marry them.

I wish!

Someone else showed up! I'm in the right place!

Are you sure it's not Nick Fury about to invite you into "The Avengers"?

Couldn't tell ya!

## ACADEMIA

---

**Ava Helmer** <AVA.HELMER@gmail.com>
to Gen

Day one complete! So far I have learned . . . nothing! Intro to Screenwriting was basically an extension of that uncomfortable orientation, and Symbols and Conceptual Systems 101 was even more confusing than its name. I'm starting to think the entire Thematic Option Honors program is just an excuse to keep the loser kids away from the jocks in regular GEs to avoid physical assault lawsuits. (Yes, I am calling myself a loser. Which is OK because in five or six years losers will be cool. At least in LA.)

I can't believe I only have two classes in an entire day! What am I supposed to do with the rest of this time? I'm used to six classes, one study hall, and a night of extracurriculars and homework. I don't do well with this much free time. I need structure. I should have signed up for 20 credits. Scratch that, I should have failed senior year and gone back to SMHS.

How was your first day? Did you uncover further corruption in the Catholic Church? *Spotlight* is begging for a sequel.

I am so bored. It's my first week of college and I'm already bored. Maybe I'll go home this weekend? My dad probably needs a tennis partner.

Your tiresome friend,

A

P.S. I think college might be a pyramid scheme. Think about it.

## Re: ACADEMIA

---

**Gen Goldman** <GENX1999@gmail.com>

to Ava

Glad to hear you are having such a great time! Make sure you pick up a book in between all those shots of Patron.

You're not boring. You're guarded and unusual and a little bit unbalanced, but you're not boring. I'm not BFF with boring people. It would ruin my highly crafted Tumblr brand.

Do you know who IS boring? Shannon. She's already obsessed with that guy from the baseball house and wants us to go back tonight. I can only handle so much hypermasculinity masquerading as heterosexuality.

My classes were fine. I think. Slept through part of Earth Science: Natural Disasters. I already know that humans survive. Unfortunately.

Don't go home this weekend. That's like admitting defeat before the Hulk even breaks your heart, Black Widow. (UGH. I hated that story line.)

Listen. I know that no one will ever compare to me, but try to make a new friend. Even if it's just to suck their blood.

Don't want to destroy you, but your dad has plenty of tennis partners. I know all about them from that one time he drove me to the DMV. Stan is the best player but Mark is the most consistent.

HUGS AND KISSES AND FEMINISM,

G

## Re: ACADEMIA

---

**Ava Helmer** <AVA.HELMER@gmail.com>

to Gen

Mark's second serve is complete shit.

**12:07PM PST**

Can I sit with total strangers in the dining hall without looking like an idiot?

Week 3? No. Week 1? Sure.

Hot blondes or nerdy engineering students?

Engineers. Think long term.

Wish me luck.

Sending you empowerment instead.

Would prefer luck.

1:13PM PST

I might have made friends!

Ask them to build you a bridge. Then you'll know for sure.

I went with the blondes.

Pussy.

## THIS IS NOT A DRILL

**Gen Goldman** <GENX1999@gmail.com>

to Ava

I did cocaine.

Before you freak out (!), please read the rest of this email and remember that I must be fine because I have the capacity to write this email.

It all started at the . . . baseball house. Yes, I went back again. Mostly as an exercise in boredom and to get Shannon out of our room. I figured I would drop her off with Mike the meaty outfielder and return to catch up on *The 100.* But, much like my horoscope predicted, Saturn was providing returns.

As soon as I entered the house, and recoiled from weed-infused BO, I saw Molly. (ICYMI, Molly is that hot bisexual girl from the first bball party.) She was already drunk and making fun of all the boys' tight pants. And I quote: "Obviously male sports is just a socially acceptable way for males to exhibit homosexual tendencies without repercussions." Most of the guys laughed it off (two of them even kissed), but Shannon's jerk Mike wasn't having it.

Molly was going to another party anyway, so we left together.

I thought I had been to parties before. Birthday parties. Bar mitzvahs. That weird lunch when your mom was elected PTA president.

I was wrong. THIS was a PAR-T.

We took the train to the South End (think WeHo) and walked a few blocks to this graduate student's apartment. Graduate students are the shit because they're stunted enough to stay students but mature enough to know how to buy drugs and not get arrested.

Molly knew everyone there, confirming my suspicions that she is the coolest person at Emerson. Which is a true accomplishment considering the co-creator of *Friends* is a professor. (Working on getting you an autograph.)

I think I finally found my people. You are my person, but these are MY PEOPLE. I think everyone there had already had sex with each other. Not at once, but MAYBE at once??

The guys acted like girls and the girls acted like they hated the guys. It was the best.

Anyway. Back to the drugs. Since I'm sure you did a CTRL+F as soon as you opened this.

Molly was in a bit of a mood from the beginning. I think that boy/girl Charlie was blowing her off, so she wanted to have fun regardless of her mental state. Apparently, cocaine has this magical ability to override all feelings. I think that must be why people are addicted to it ;)

After two shots of vodka, Molly wanted more. Not more shots. Thank God. Vodka is terrible. You would hate it. It tastes like nail polish remover smells.

Anywayyyyyy. I'm talking to this guy about self-driving cars (they're happening, FYI) when Molly appears with this grin on her face. She wants to go to the bathroom. Together. Cue PERKS OF BEING A WALLFLOWER MUSIC.

We patiently wait in this long line so we can do our coke like polite people. But when we finally get inside, the last thing we want to do is inhale. (Classic Gen poop joke! I will never outgrow these.) We were still committed to the cocaine. Actually, I don't know if I was committed or just going with the flow. Molly could have pulled out two Ring Pops and I would have been equally down.

But it wasn't Ring Pops. It was cocaine, and Molly spread it out on the counter delicately, perfectly dividing it with her student ID. It was very sweet. She then asked me for a dollar bill because we are lit but not like fifty-dollar-bill cocaine lit. Yet.

She went first and then I dive-bombed into a life of seedy glamour. I think I am now addicted to cocaine and will proceed to use all of my life's saving to procure more of it even if I have to sell my body.

JUST KIDDING. It sucked.

It didn't suck, but it wasn't much of anything. My teeth felt numb and I couldn't go to bed until 5. I talked a bit faster but I wasn't any smarter.

Overall, I would give cocaine 2 stars.

Gen

P.S. I looked it up and the cocaine import business is awful. I am now a cocaine conscientious objector.

**7:32 AM PST**

Call me.

GEN!!

## Re: THIS IS NOT A DRILL

---

**Ava Helmer** <AVA.HELMER@gmail.com>

to Gen

I can't believe you didn't answer my four calls. Either you are in class or too ashamed of your hooligan actions to face me.

Also, are you insane? Emerson is clearly reading your emails and now they have proof that you've snorted Cherry Cola. (This is a code word.)

Why are you doing this? Is this a cry for help?

I knew your dysfunctional family was going to have a long-term impact on your life, but I thought it wouldn't become apparent until later when you'd already made a name for yourself at some journal and had a small nest egg. (Remember to invest. Otherwise your money is just sitting around.)

To be fair, I called you the first three times before I finished reading the email and still thought you were a blossoming addict. Now I am a bit calmer, but DON'T FOR ONE SECOND THINK YOU CAN PULL THIS SHIT AGAIN! Cherry Cola is dangerous! Your mind is a precious vessel that carries all of my most favorite thoughts and feelings. You must protect it at all costs.

Do whatever you want with your body.

A

**Re: THIS IS NOT A DRILL**

**Gen Goldman** <GENX1999@gmail.com>

to Ava

Hahahahahahahahahaha

No one is reading my emails. And we joke about drugs all the time. #meth

**Re: THIS IS NOT A DRILL**

**Ava Helmer** <AVA.HELMER@gmail.com>

to Gen

It's almost like you didn't make me watch the Edward Snowden documentary four times.

**Re: THIS IS NOT A DRILL**

**Gen Goldman** <GENX1999@gmail.com>

to Ava

#celebritycrush

**2:34 PM PST**

I almost beat my dad. 4–6!

You went home????

My parents needed me. I'm the glue that holds them together.

Also my dorm's laundry room makes my clothes dirtier.

So send your clothes out! And make out on a washer!

With who? Myself?

Love URself. 😉 ♪

I'd rather go home.

Hard to masturbate there. Fo sho.

**10:17 PM EST**

Creep alert!

I was just liking your photos! You don't want me to like your photos?!

No! Not that!

Please like all my photos.

I ran into Grabby Igor.

Noooooooooooo

Did he grab you?

Almost immediately.

He's a sophomore at BU.

He has a GF.

WHAT!

You have to save her! She must be brainwashed!

I tried to give her signals (wink once for help, wink twice for Mace), but she seemed to actually like him?????

Grabby Igor has a girlfriend and I'm at home with my parents.

You CHOSE to be at home with your parents.

Go grab someone.

Maybe.

## CRAZY IDEA

---

**Ava Helmer** <AVA.HELMER@gmail.com>

to Gen

I think I must be losing my mind (again, I know), but what would you say if I tried to join a sorority?

Actually. I know what you'll say. So I have prepared a rebuttal. With the dual purpose of simultaneously convincing myself that this is not my worst idea since joining that middle-age pottery class.

**1) Gross**

a. Yes. The very idea of a sorority is gross. Paying for friends. Reinforcing the gender binary. Heels. BUT isn't feminism about reclaiming our lives and supporting each other? Isn't a sorority the original safe space?

**2) The people**

a. Again, yes. Most sorority girls are stereotypically vapid or, worse, pretending to be vapid. But USC has such a strong Greek culture that basically everyone here is

rushing and not everyone can be a complete loser. Right?? Statistically that can't be possible.
b. Elizabeth Banks, Lucy Liu, and Julia Louis-Dreyfus were all in sororities! (Thanks, BuzzFeed.)

**3) The mandatory parties**
a. Right. The parties. This is the hardest thing for me to wrap my brain around, but I think I need to start viewing my social life as a requirement instead of an option. Being part of a house will give me a weird structure whereby I know what parties to attend, when to attend them, and who to attend them with. If any of the socials have ice cream it almost seems bearable!

**4) It's a sorority**
a. Right. Please see above.

In other news, Jessica had sex in our room last Thursday while I was also in the room. That's the real reason I went home. I was just too mortified to say it or type it until this moment.

I HEARD SEX! IT SOUNDS WEIRD!

Ava

**Re: CRAZY IDEA**

---

**Gen Goldman** <GENX1999@gmail.com>

to Ava

Did you watch? I bet you watched.

Congrats on your first threesome.

**Re: CRAZY IDEA**

---

**Ava Helmer** <AVA.HELMER@gmail.com>

to Gen

That's all you took from my email????

**Re: CRAZY IDEA**

---

**Ava Helmer** <AVA.HELMER@gmail.com>

to Gen

AND EVERYTHING I SAW WAS AGAINST MY WILL.

## Re: CRAZY IDEA

**Gen Goldman** <GENX1999@gmail.com>

to Ava

You'll be fine. I once saw my mom going down on my dad, and I'm still around to talk about it. (The cocaine addiction helps.)

I was mulling over my response regarding this "hypothetical sorority."

I think you should do it. If you hate it, you'll quit. And if you love it, we have to stop being friends. But you won't even notice because you'll be so immersed in the sisterhood.

Kappa Alpha Puke!

I'm proud of you.

G

P.S. Don't let them circle your fat with a Sharpie.

**Re: CRAZY IDEA**

---

**Ava Helmer** <AVA.HELMER@gmail.com>

to Gen

Really? That's it? I'm not going to have to convince you with a series of long emails, GIFs, and links to *The House Bunny*?

I'm starting to think you don't care about me anymore.

**Re: CRAZY IDEA**

---

**Gen Goldman** <GENX1999@gmail.com>

to Ava

New email. Who dis?

## Re: CRAZY IDEA

---

**Gen Goldman** <GENX1999@gmail.com>

to Ava

JK TIMES 1,000!

I DO care about you. That's why I want you to go out there and make mistakes. (Like joining a sorority.)

I want hot pics from your fall mixer.

## Re: CRAZY IDEA

---

**Ava Helmer** <AVA.HELMER@gmail.com>

to Gen

You're bad at being supportive.

**6:12 PM EST**

Send me that paper you wrote last year on "Gender Politics in Soviet Russia."

Why?

I'm gonna turn it in.

Go away.

**SOS**

---

**Ava Helmer** <AVA.HELMER@gmail.com>

to Gen

Just had my first therapy session. USC gave me a therapist in training. I've been in therapy longer than she has been a therapist.

OY

**Re: SOS**

---

**Gen Goldman** <GENX1999@gmail.com>

to Ava

Did you give her your streamlined "This is what is wrong with me and this is how we have to fix it"?

**Re: SOS**

---

**Ava Helmer** <AVA.HELMER@gmail.com>

to Gen

Yes. And she just nodded. Looks like I'm going to have to therapize myself.

POOF! I'm no longer afraid of dirt or consumed with obsessive thoughts!

I'm pretty much an X-Man.

## Re: SOS

**Gen Goldman** <GENX1999@gmail.com>

to Ava

It's X-MEN.

Congrats on such a speedy recovery.

4:37 PM EST

How can you tell if someone is hitting on you?

HA! You sent this to Ava.

I know. But I need help. This TA asked me to come to her office hours.

You are in school. That is a normal thing. Send a smoke signal if she invites you to her bedroom.

Copy.

Did you already fail something?

TBD.

## OLDER WOMEN

**Gen Goldman** <GENX1999@gmail.com>

to Ava

Is there a time machine available for private use? I know I should probably use it to kill Hitler or something, but I sort of just want to blast forward into my late 20s. Maybe even 30 if I don't get crow's feet.

Charlotte (my TA) is a goddess. I can't pin her exact age, but it's somewhere past caring what people think and a few years before being completely out of touch with current music. She works nights at the *Globe* news desk and has her own police radio. Basically a real-life superhero.

Turns out, I am not failing anything. I am doing the opposite of failing. I am standing out. Which is extra hard since most of my classmates have neon hair.

Charlotte called me into her office to tell me I should start writing for the *Beacon* (school newspaper). She was the editor in chief during her undergrad and apparently, "Classes are for parents. The *Beacon* is for journalists."

The first meeting of the year is tonight. I'm going to wear a blazer and not smile once. Charlotte said she would copyedit my first few assignments. Just so I don't make a complete ass of myself.

Finally someone around here appreciates my God-given gift for the written word.

MEEP!

G

P.S. Please do not point out my embargo on extracurricular activities. This counts more like an internship. With actual bylines your mom can print out.

## Re: OLDER WOMEN

**Ava Helmer** <AVA.HELMER@gmail.com>

to Gen

As I live and breathe, Genevieve Goldman has become a company man! Congratulations on having a goal and following through with it! (Maybe I shouldn't jinx it. Not exactly sure what time the meeting is.)

I think writing for the *Beacon* (established 1881 with notable alums including Thomas Jefferson and Genevieve Goldman) is a great idea! It's so important for you to be involved in something other than drugs.

Charlotte sounds like the perfect kind of arrogant to be a good mentor. Just don't overstay your welcome during those office hours. She probably has a lot of older woman stuff to do, like moisturizing her elbows.

## Re: OLDER WOMEN

**Gen Goldman** <GENX1999@gmail.com>

to Ava

Do people really moisturize their elbows?

## Re: OLDER WOMEN

**Ava Helmer** <AVA.HELMER@gmail.com>

to Gen

Oh, yeah! Moisture is the first line of defense against aging! That's why I'm always so slippery.

**7:42 PM EST**

There are only 3 women on staff here.

One is the lifestyle editor and the other 2 are copy editors.

Are you going to strike?

Not yet. Have to infiltrate from the inside first. And buy a hat.

Why a hat?

NEWSIES

G2G

Seize the day!

Number disconnected.

5:29 PM PST

Did you get the photo?

Which one? You sent 12.

I'm panicking.

Can I pull off yellow? Or do I look like a ghost?

Imagine if you were a ghost this whole time. That would be so cool.

GEN! My first rush event is in one hour! Now is not the time!

The red dress. Lucky photo number 7.

THANK YOU.

I knew it.

**GO GREEK!**

---

**Ava Helmer** <AVA.HELMER@gmail.com>

to Gen

Imagine fifty blond girls singing "hello" to you while you're ushered into a mini-mansion surrounded by twenty other overwhelmed freshmen and one sophomore who couldn't get into a house last year.

BECAUSE THAT WAS MY DAY.

And to think I had social anxiety before.

The best way I could describe rushing is a mixture of

speed dating and job interviews. (Not that I have ever done either really.)

The girls talk to you as a group and then you get broken up into duos where you have to act like being a Kappa Kappa Gamma has been your dream since childhood even though you just learned the name Kappa Kappa Gamma two hours ago.

The entire concept is elitist and hierarchical and I MUST GET IN. I know. It's pathetic. But that's just human nature. As soon as you are told something is hard to get, you want it more. Like when you wanted to date Joel Simpson even though he was SUPER gay.

I don't think I made a complete fool of myself, but it's impossible to tell because all the girls were smiling the whole time. Yes. The entire time. I think they must do some sort of cheek exercise during prerush week. Yes. That is a thing. I can only imagine that it involves a lot of dieting and hand-holding.

Anyway. I went to five of the ten houses today. I do the second half tomorrow. And then I put down my top five choices and they put down their top choices and then maybe there is some crossover? If not, I get stuck going to the shitty houses, which will lead to a lifetime of shame and regret. I know it's 2017, but if I don't get called back to Delta Gamma at least once, I'm going to yell anti-Semitism.

My head is spinning. It's like college applications all over again but compacted into one day without the luxury of hiding behind your computer screen.

What if no one picks me at all? I'll be fine if I don't make it into the best house by the end or end up with my third choice, but what if I don't even get into the second round??? I asked my rush adviser if this is possible and she said it's never happened before.

Until now.

Ava

## Re: GO GREEK!

---

**Gen Goldman** <GENX1999@gmail.com>

to Ava

Remember when you thought you weren't going to get into USC?

Remember when you thought you weren't going to get into the film school at USC?

Remember when you thought you weren't going to get into a stupid f-ing sorority at USC?

If you have short-term memory loss, will you tell me?

Any one of these faux sisterhoods would be lucky to have you. And if they can't see that IMMEDIATELY, they will regret it when you're accepting an Oscar for best original screenplay about a sorority that's secretly a terrorist cell. (That's good! You can use that.)

Take a deep breath. Loofah all your anxiety away and remember that every awful moment becomes a great story later.

ALSO, you have the benefit of fictionalizing your life. I just report the news.

**11:39 PM EST**

How's it going?

My mouth hurts.

From smiling? Or sucking D?

Why would I have to "suck D" to get into a sorority full of women?

Gender is not confined to sex organs.

Have you learned nothing from me?

I've been rushing for two days and I'm already dumber.

## FUCK ME

---

**Gen Goldman** <GENX1999@gmail.com>

to Ava

So, I'm sorry to throw this at you during what I can only imagine is a tumultuous time where women sit around and judge you on shallow aspects of your looks and personality, but I am officially in crisis.

I got my first assignment for the news desk and . . . It's

not pretty. There's a new dean of communications. My editor, Kent, told me to call him up and write a fluff piece. He didn't say "fluff piece," but that's basically the same as "profile." But then I open up my stupid laptop, because you've turned me into an overachiever, and I Google the guy. That's it. That's all I do. A quick Google. To see if maybe he plays the ukulele? Or some other innocent hobby I can put in the profile.

What comes up?

A SEXUAL HARASSMENT LAWSUIT

That's right! The guy was booted from his last job for groping a student, and my dumb-ass college hired him.

Does our HR department never get to the third page of Google?

So now I have to decide if I should be a whistle-blower or not. Should I ask this creep about the lawsuit, or should I focus on the ukulele?

HELP!

Did I mention that the interview is in 1 hour?

**Re: FUCK ME**

---

**Ava Helmer** <AVA.HELMER@gmail.com>
to Gen

While I love that you come to me for advice and guidance, maybe you should be asking your editor these questions instead?

Also, ew. The real world is awful.

**Re: FUCK ME**

---

**Gen Goldman** <GENX1999@gmail.com>
to Ava

YOU'RE A GENIUS.

P.S. I might have thrown up.

**Re: FUCK ME**

---

**Gen Goldman** <GENX1999@gmail.com>
to Ava

UPDATE! This is my Watergate.

My editor, Kent, started whooping when I showed him the article. Apparently nothing interesting has happened on this campus since the theater school put on *Miss Saigon* with all white kids.

They want me to go about the interview as though it's a standard fluff piece (this time Kent, my editor, actually said "fluff piece") and then BAM. Hit him with the lawsuit question.

I'm freaking out but I think in a good way.

Will report back. (See what I did there?)

Genevieve Goldman
Investigative Journalist

## Re: FUCK ME

---

**Ava Helmer** <AVA.HELMER@gmail.com>

to Gen

Remember me when you're giving TED Talks.

**Re: FUCK ME**

---

**Gen Goldman** <GENX1999@gmail.com>

to Ava

Holy shit. He freaked out. He started denying everything and called the girl a hussy. A HUSSY. Can you believe it? I'm basically Rachel Maddow right now, and the year is 1955.

Kent, my editor, wants the entire article to be a take-down piece attacking our administration for allowing a known predator among female students. 500 words. On the cover. Maybe more on the website.

I'm gonna ask Charlotte for help. It's due in 2 days.

Pray for me.

**Re: FUCK ME**

---

**Ava Helmer** <AVA.HELMER@gmail.com>

to Gen

I just prayed to every "known" entity. But you don't need organized religion. You just need you!

I'm crying a little bit. I'm either really proud or really hungry.

10:14 AM PST

What's a good song to listen to when you're depressed but don't like sad music?

"Fuck You" by Lily Allen.

You OK?

TBD.

## THE COMPLETE MORTIFICATION OF AVA HELMER (1999–PRESENT)

---

**Ava Helmer** <AVA.HELMER@gmail.com>
to Gen

1) Birth. I poop inside my mom's womb. I obviously don't remember this. But I do remember all the times my mom talked about it at family events.

2) Kindergarten. I try to sit on the teacher's lap during naptime. She tells me that is inappropriate. In front of the entire class.

3) Third grade. Becky Olsberg and Laura Jenner invite me over for a playdate. We share secrets. I confess that sometimes I eat flowers. They tell everyone that I am secretly a horse trapped in a girl's body.

4) All of middle school.

5) Jordan F. asks me to come over to his house to ask me about you. (Did I ever tell you this? I knew you hated

Jordan F. so I might have kept that as a silent shame until now. Oh, no. What if you DIDN'T hate Jordan F. and I ruined your one shot at true happiness as well as any chance of you staying in California for college? He goes to Stanford. I love him so much.)

6) Prom. You remember.

7) Day 3 of rushing. When I find out that only 3 of 10 houses want me back. EVEN THOUGH THE AVERAGE IS 7! Only getting asked back to 3 houses in the second round is unheard of. I'm mortified.

  a. One of those houses, Pi Phi, is like the COOLEST house on campus, so they have obviously just invited me back to be nice. Or as a cruel joke. (Please refer to #3 above.)

I don't even want to go back to rush. If I do, I'll feel like I'm asking for it. (Not sexually; I know women can't actually do that.)

I want to cry, but stupid Jessica won't leave the room!

A dead person, formerly known as Ava Beth Helmer

P.S. I'm already crying. Just really softly.

**Re: THE COMPLETE MORTIFICATION OF AVA HELMER (1999–PRESENT)**

---

**Gen Goldman** <GENX1999@gmail.com>

to Ava

Are you kidding me???? I could have been married to Jordan F. by now?

My last name could have been Facker?

I'm never speaking to you again after this utter betrayal.

**Re: THE COMPLETE MORTIFICATION OF AVA HELMER (1999–PRESENT)**

---

**Gen Goldman** <GENX1999@gmail.com>

to Ava

JK JK. You told me about that Jordan F. thing immediately after it happened. You cried on the way home and I bought you fro-yo. Honestly, I'm the most hurt you don't remember the fro-yo. I asked for whipped cream and everything.

Take a deep breath and remember: college students are idiots. You wouldn't trust these girls to make you a coffee, why would you trust their character assessment?

Also, you got asked back to 3 houses! And 1 is cool?! Which is a shock to me because I assumed all sororities are inherently UNCOOL!

Maybe this Pie Phi house is the coolest because they have the smartest girls, and those smart girls are about to see how insanely awesome you are. Ever thought of that? *Harry Potter* was rejected 8 times before Bloomsbury published one of the greatest gifts to Muggle kind.

Never give up. Never surrender.

(Unless you realize sororities are lame and YOU don't want to be a part of THEM.)

Gen

P.S. Now I really want fro-yo.

**Re: THE COMPLETE MORTIFICATION OF AVA HELMER (1999–PRESENT)**

---

**Ava Helmer** <AVA.HELMER@gmail.com>
to Gen

I just found out that Jessica was rejected from Pi Phi. This somehow makes me feel better.

I am a bad person.

But a bad person who wasn't rejected from Pi Phi. (Yet.)

A

8:52 PM EST

Did you know that they make vinegar pie?

And avocado pie?

I would stay away from green grape pie.
Seems like a choking hazard.

. . .

Some conversation topics if you run out of
things to say at the pie house.

You are not helping.

I love pie!!!!!!!!!!

## I AM NOT WORTHY

---

**Gen Goldman** <GENX1999@gmail.com>

to Ava

Have I mentioned that Charlotte is a goddess? I emailed her my first draft of the article and she completely tore it to shreds. I went to her apartment to go over the edits and realized that I know absolutely nothing about writing a good story.

I buried the fucking lede! Even Midwestern moms know not to do that!

Her vocabulary is insane. Also, word flow. Who knew how much that mattered? I thought reporting was all fact, period, fact, period. NOT THE CASE. She gave me a book by Adrian Nicole LeBlanc that reads like fiction. I'll be an artist yet!

I spent 2 hours with her. Redlining. It felt like 5 minutes.

I think this article might be really good. Like good enough to get me in trouble. And maybe a spot on the staff. Waiting to hear back from my editor, Kent. But I'll be shocked if he doesn't love it. It's insanely provocative.

Did you know you can use wine corks to make a vision board? Well, you can. And it looks awesome.

Charlotte=goddess

G

## Re: I AM NOT WORTHY

---

**Ava Helmer** <AVA.HELMER@gmail.com>

to Gen

I get it. You hate Charlotte.

I can't wait to read this thing! I hope it brings down the entire establishment and Emerson folds and you move home and attend USC's prestigious Annenberg School for Communication and Journalism.

Couple of things.

1) Why did you go to her apartment? Is that allowed? Seems weird. Especially the vision board.

2) I know your editor is named Kent. But you can keep referring to him as your editor, Kent, if it makes you feel cool.

SO PROUD! My little rebel is growing up.

Ava

**9:24 AM EST**

Greetings from inside my Earth Science teacher's bathroom. Taking a shower.

I can't tell if you're joking.

Emerson is VERY liberal.

Ooooooo! A loofah!

Picture or it didn't happen.

DrOPeD PhONe iN WaTEr.

CaN NOt CoMpUTe.

## ROUND TWO BITCHES

---

**Ava Helmer** <AVA.HELMER@gmail.com>
to Gen

Do I sound like a Pi Phi yet? Don't worry. None of them actually talk like that. Or if some of them do, they're kept in the back during rush.

Got the results from round two and ALL three houses asked me back! I'm officially caught up! You're allowed a maximum of three houses for Sisterhood Day. (Remember that month I ignored your obsession with *Fuller House?* Please do me the same courtesy with Sisterhood Day.)

I feel high. Or what I imagine high to feel like. God damn, it feels good to be wanted. (In a nonsexual way, by a bunch of college girls who love to DIY.)

In related news, I think I have made an actual film school friend. Her name is Sophia and she's in my Introduction to Cinema class. Her mom is from Portugal and her dad is from Mexico but she grew up in New York, which already makes her 100 times more interesting than me. She wants to write international thrillers, so already I don't understand our blossoming friendship. I think she might be one of those people who say "You're funny" without actually laughing. Her boyfriend is at NYU so I think she is bored and lonely. I can relate to bored and lonely! We've already eaten lunch together three times and one dinner followed by a movie. I don't want to count my chickens before they hatch, but I think she likes me.

If I believed in bullshit astrology, I'd think Mercury was in retrograde or something!

Ava

## Re: ROUND TWO BITCHES

---

**Gen Goldman** <GENX1999@gmail.com>

to Ava

Mercury in retrograde is a bad thing. I think the phenomenon you're thinking of is caused by Saturn returning. Though it's a bit early for that. According to all the bullshit I very much believe in.

This is all great news! And just days after "The Complete Mortification of Ava Helmer (1999–Present)"! I knew it was too early to publish! You have so much life and mortification ahead!

Maybe one day a small baby will shit inside YOU!

Sophia sounds cool? I don't like people who don't laugh. What are they hiding? Other than a really obnoxious laugh?

I do like people who grew up in NYC. She can continue to give you that dose of edge that you are missing now that I'm gone. What's the deal with the BF? Are they open? Everyone at Emerson is open. It's wild. But makes a lot of biological sense.

Too bad Patrick insisted on monogamy for those two months we "dated" junior year. I could have had a lot of fun with his teammates.

Going out with Molly again tonight. Will try my best not to get high on Cherry Cola.

XOXO & EQUALITY.

Gen

8:59 PM PST

What's 24 times 57?

I have no fucking idea.

Good. A high-on-Cherry-Cola Gen would have just guessed.

Be safe! ♥

1,743

**LIKE A CHIC-A-CHERRY COLA**

---

**Gen Goldman** <GENX1999@gmail.com>

to Ava

Greetings from the ER. My stomach was successfully pumped. Most of my brain cells should return in the next 7–8 years. Or did they say months? Too damaged to remember.

Did you believe that at all? Probably for a second. Or, knowing you, you still believe it and are calling all the ERs in the Boston area.

To recap: I'm fine. Molly and I got a little drunk and silly, but other than that it was an early night. Shannon was out with an infielder to make that outfielder jealous, so we just came back to my room around midnight to watch *Doctor Who.* She had never seen it before so I showed her "Vincent and the Doctor."

We both cried.

## Re: LIKE A CHIC-A-CHERRY COLA

---

**Ava Helmer** <AVA.HELMER@gmail.com>

to Gen

She had never seen *Doctor Who* before?? I thought we liked this girl.

Remember last summer when you made me watch the entire reboot? I don't. Because I was asleep.

I'm glad that your dalliance into hard cola has finished. Now you still have war stories but all of your teeth.

In Greek news, I just found out I'm still in the running for house of pies! Today is the last event (Preference Day) and then tomorrow we get our bids. There is a rumor that all the fraternity boys hold up signs to rank our attractiveness as we run to our new house, but I have to assume that started from some teen comedy and not real life. (PLEASE LET ME GET ABOVE A 6!)

Sophia from screenwriting thinks sororities are dumb, which honestly makes me like her more.

Go, Trojans! (Just testing it out. I hear football games are mandatory.)

Ava

**9:01 PM EST**

Kent, my aforementioned editor, LOVES the story. It's going front page tomorrow! 😬

🎉

Send me the link!

## MY LAST WILL AND TESTEMENT

---

**Ava Helmer** <AVA.HELMER@gmail.com>

to Gen

I will never eat a slice of pie again. Which will probably be easy since I plan to take my own life. (I know you've said that formerly suicidal teens aren't allowed to make suicide jokes, but fuck you, this is all I have.)

Spoiler alert: I DIDN'T GET INTO PI PHI.

I received a bid from stupid Gamma Phi instead. Which is like the second to worst house on the row.

I'm honestly embarrassed to ask my parents to pay for such lame friends.

**10:42 PM EST**

Still alive? 💀

For now.

Gamma Phi. Pi Phi. Seems pretty similar.

You don't understand. They're all losers.

How?

They're lame.

But why?

BECAUSE THEY'RE LOSERS

Ava.

I'M A LOSER NOW TOO

Awwwww

You were always a loser.

The votes hadn't been officially tallied.

You're crazy.

Call me whenever my nonclassist best friend returns.

SEE YOU NEVER

**MEA CULPA**

---

**Ava Helmer** <AVA.HELMER@gmail.com>

to Gen

Hi. This is your former best friend, Ava, who briefly lost her mind yesterday and turned into a horrible judgmental monster. The original Ava is back, albeit ashamed.

I'm not going to say that the girls in Gamma Phi aren't losers, but I will apologize for calling them that. So aggressively. In all caps.

I decided to attend Bid Night mostly because I wanted to save face in front of Jessica, who got into Kappa, which was her first choice the whole time. (Roommates are the worst.)

I showed up at the house and everyone was so goddamn excited. They must have had short-term memory loss, because I guarantee at least half of them wanted a bid from a different house an hour ago. Anyway, I felt like I had to fake it too, and within 30 minutes I had tricked myself into feeling something close to happiness. (I think this must be how sororities work. Fake smiles/behavioral conditioning/Stockholm syndrome.)

We were all given identical tank tops and told to put them on. Even though I'd been wearing a long-sleeved shirt because the desert is cold at night. I had to stuff my shirt in my purse and walk around with that ridiculous blue bra you made me buy showing.

After so many hugs with people I was not ready to touch, the partying began. Not at the house, because you can't party at sororities, but at our brother fraternity, ZBT. (I can't believe I just said OUR. The Kool-Aid goes down quick.)

We arrived at ZBT to a line of freshman pledges handing out tropical punch and leis. The party had a jungle theme and probably at least one case of date rape. (I'm joking. I hope.)

I didn't take the punch because, obviously, but I did take a beer, since it comes sealed.

It. Was. Awful. How do people drink more than one of them at a time? DISGUSTING.

Overall, it was an experience. A bona fide college experience. I even stayed past midnight. (12:05 to be exact.)

I would rate the night 3 out of 5 stars.

I hope you can forgive me and see that I have changed. Or changed back.

Ava

P.S. I met a cute boy and we talked alone for 20 minutes but it probably meant nothing.

## Re: MEA CULPA

**Gen Goldman** <GENX1999@gmail.com>

to Ava

WHAT HAVE I TOLD YOU ABOUT BURYING THE LEDE?!

Who is the boy?? How cute is he??? What does his dick look like??

If you don't answer two of those questions I will never forgive you for turning into Regina George yesterday.

I'm glad you're giving the losers a second chance. Imagine if I hadn't given you one ;)

Also: "New Dean of Communications Failed to Communicate His Past"

G

## DEAR MISS CAPOTE

**Ava Helmer** <AVA.HELMER@gmail.com>

to Gen

Your article was . . . AMAZING. So biting yet objective. I felt like I was presented with facts and then left to draw my own conclusion. The conclusion being: this guy needs to get fired!

OH MY GOD! Imagine if you get that guy fired. That would be so impressive. I think I would pass out from the guilt, but you have a better constitution than me.

Wow! Just wow!

"It brings into question the great lengths the administration goes to selecting its student body versus the lax vetting of its faculty."

BOOYAH!

I'm sending it to my entire family. Your parents will want to read it too. (I hope. I never know what to expect from them.)

You deserve an award. I'll look for one on Etsy.

Your secret admirer,

Ava

**Re: DEAR MISS CAPOTE**

---

**Gen Goldman** <GENX1999@gmail.com>
to Ava

TELL ME ABOUT THE BOY BEFORE I STRANGLE YOU.

**Re: DEAR MISS CAPOTE**

---

**Ava Helmer** <AVA.HELMER@gmail.com>
to Gen

Hahahaha

Sorry. I don't know what to say because I don't know if the entire thing was in my head. I guess I will start by setting the scene.

Did I mention I'm currently in Screenwriting 101?

The night: black. The stars: I'm not sure. We were inside.

I was sort of hanging back, taking it all in, possibly planning an escape, when the guy, Jake, started talking to me. Apparently he's a sophomore production major who recognized me from the film school Coffee Bean.

Is it insane that this is the most flattered I have EVER been? I mean it's not an inherently good thing to be recognized. I recognize awful people all of the time, but he probably wouldn't have talked to me if he recognized me for being awful, right?

I think the conversation went well? It was pretty standard. Where you from? What do you like to watch? Will you have my baby? (I think I just implied the last thing with my eyes.)

I don't know. I don't know how to interpret boy stuff without you watching it and interpreting it for me.

Although, come to think of it, none of your interpretations have been particularly helpful either.

I must be a lost cause.

Don't look for me.

## Re: DEAR MISS CAPOTE

---

**Gen Goldman** <GENX1999@gmail.com>

to Ava

That got dark. REAL fast.

I need more details. How did the conversation end? What is his Instagram?

**Re: DEAR MISS CAPOTE**

---

**Ava Helmer** <AVA.HELMER@gmail.com>

to Gen

I don't know his Instagram. Or his last name. Night ended with him being called off to play beer pong by one of his brothers. He told me to watch, but I said I had to go home because I need a lot of sleep to maintain a balanced mental state.

**Re: DEAR MISS CAPOTE**

---

**Ava Helmer** <AVA.HELMER@gmail.com>

to Gen

I'M A LOSER! I DON'T EVEN DESERVE TO BE A GAMMA PHI!

**Re: DEAR MISS CAPOTE**

---

**Gen Goldman** <GENX1999@gmail.com>

to Ava

Is this him?

Instagram.com/chinatownjake98

## Re: DEAR MISS CAPOTE

**Ava Helmer** <AVA.HELMER@gmail.com>

to Gen

How did you do that????? And why are you using your powers to find frat boys on Instagram?

## Re: DEAR MISS CAPOTE

**Gen Goldman** <GENX1999@gmail.com>

to Ava

Unfortunately, my superpowers start and end at finding frat boys on Instagram. That's why I keep getting rejected from Xavier's School for Gifted Youngsters.

Follow him.

## Re: DEAR MISS CAPOTE

**Ava Helmer** <AVA.HELMER@gmail.com>

to Gen

Absolutely not. But I bow down to your craft.

**3:42 PM PST**

Oh my god. The funniest thing just happened.

Spit take?

Banana peel?

Pie in the face?

Oh, no! Forget I said pie!

Hahaha

Your sense of humor is atrocious.

Was it a farcical case of mistaken identity?

Kind of!

I knew it.

## A FARCICAL CASE OF MISTAKEN IDENTITY

**Ava Helmer** <AVA.HELMER@gmail.com>
to Gen

SO! In an attempt to ease us into the craft of screenwriting, we've been writing prose this whole time in Screenwriting 101. Please don't bother to point out the irony. It's already eating me alive.

Anywho, this last assignment was a first-person short story with the option of being autobiographical. I chose to write fiction because nothing exciting has ever happened to me. Unless you count starting Prozac at age four. But toddlers aren't reliable narrators and I'm not a good enough writer to tackle that yet.

I end up writing this quirky account of a high school boy

having his first kiss with a girl and realizing that he is actually gay. Except I never explicitly say that it's from the point of view of a boy AND I never give him a name because it's written in the first person. What ends up happening?

Everyone in my class thinks I chose to write an autobiographical story. And not just any autobiographical story. My autobiographical COMING OUT story. Hahahaha.

The entire class thought I was gay for a few days until we went over my story and I started getting notes.

So funny and embarrassing! I had to assure everyone I'm not gay, just an unclear writer.

Hope you're drinking something while reading this, so you get to spit take!

A

**Re: A FARCICAL CASE OF MISTAKEN IDENTITY**

---

**Gen Goldman** <GENX1999@gmail.com>

to Ava

I don't understand. What is so funny about people thinking you are gay?

## Re: A FARCICAL CASE OF MISTAKEN IDENTITY

**Ava Helmer** <AVA.HELMER@gmail.com>
to Gen

I don't know! It just seemed ridiculous. No one has ever thought I was gay. I'm like a virginal Charlotte York with a bigger nose.

**2:15 PM PST**

Jake is two people in front of me at the Coffee Bean!

What do I do?

He's ordering! I can't tell if he saw me!

GEN!!!!!!

**5:27 PM PST**

If you're dead, I hope you left me your leather jacket.

I can't pull it off, but I'll hang it in my house.

As art.

Hello????

**8:42 PM PST**

Sry. Busy.

Doing what?

Kissing girls

. . .

Oh my god. Do you actually think I'm homophobic?

My aunt is gay!

Not openly, but we all know.

K.

Gen! Come on! Are you seriously mad?

Talk l8r.

**PRIDE**

---

**Ava Helmer** <AVA.HELMER@gmail.com>

to Gen

Dearest Genevieve,

I offer my sincerest apologies to the gay, lesbian, bisexual, and transgender community. I had no intention of offending any of our queer friends, family, or loved ones. There is absolutely nothing wrong with appearing gay or actually being gay. In fact, I felt a bit honored that my peers thought I was cool enough to get a hot girl to kiss me behind the bleachers.

I have no excuse for my blunder, but please keep in mind that USC is not the enlightened campus Emerson is, and I am a bit behind in my evolution of tolerance and sensitivity.

In conclusion, I have nothing but the upmost respect for Kristen Stewart, Neil Patrick Harris, and Laverne Cox, among many other notable LGBT icons. I will spend the rest of my living days making it up to them.

(That said, I take a bit of offense that you would jump to a homophobic conclusion about me. I was equally taken aback that time someone thought I was Russian. Also, I know your MO is avoidance, but it's sort of impossible when you live 3,000 miles away and I can't just show up at your house and force you to talk to me.)

All the love in the world,

Ava Helmer
(No homo)

## Re: PRIDE

**Gen Goldman** <GENX1999@gmail.com>
to Ava

Hey. I'm sorry I went MIA like that. I just . . . didn't love your reaction, but I'm sure I read too much into it or something.

I think I'm just juggling a lot of things. The article is getting a bunch of attention (bad and good), and I haven't been keeping up with homework because of all the *Beacon* stuff.

Plus. I've been hooking up with someone and it's taking up a lot of my brain space.

So I probably overreacted. NBD. Thanks for being the bigger person and yada yada.

G

**Re: PRIDE**

---

**Ava Helmer** <AVA.HELMER@gmail.com>

to Gen

WHO ARE HOOKING UP WITH???? ARE YOU HAVING SEX??? WHAT IS GOING ON???

**11:04 AM PST**

WHO ARE YOU HOOKING UP WITH???

Think about it.

IT'S ALL I'M THINKING ABOUT.

😇

OK.

I figured it out.

Kent, your editor.

HAHAHAHAHA

Are you laughing because I'm so right or because I'm so wrong?

Wrong.

And adorable.

OK. That's fine. You shouldn't be hooking up with your editor anyway . . .

Hmmmm. What other guys have you mentioned?

You're getting colder.

???

It's not a guy.

Hello?

. . . .

Molly!

Yes.

Second guess. Pretty good.

## SHOULD WE TALK ABOUT THIS?

**Ava Helmer** <AVA.HELMER@gmail.com>
to Gen

I wrote out a bunch of different versions of this email, but I think the subject line says it all.

Ava

## Re: SHOULD WE TALK ABOUT THIS?

**Gen Goldman** <GENX1999@gmail.com>
to Ava

Nope. I'm good.

## Re: SHOULD WE TALK ABOUT THIS?

**Ava Helmer** <AVA.HELMER@gmail.com>

to Gen

OK, well, I'm not good. You realized that you are gay and didn't bother to tell me? Your best friend in the entire world? Or is Molly your best friend now? Are you even in Boston? You've stopped geo-tagging all your posts. Have you changed your name and moved to Zimbabwe? Because I feel completely abandoned in this moment.

TO BE CLEAR: I have NO problem with you being gay. I have a problem with you not telling me. And yes, that is a selfish problem, but I am a selfish person.

## Re: SHOULD WE TALK ABOUT THIS?

**Gen Goldman** <GENX1999@gmail.com>

to Ava

This is why I didn't want to tell you. I'm not gay. I'm hooking up with a girl. Not everything is black and white.

## Re: SHOULD WE TALK ABOUT THIS?

**Ava Helmer** <AVA.HELMER@gmail.com>

to Gen

Wow. OK. That was super condescending. Especially since you know it's hard for me to not see things in black and white BECAUSE OF MY MENTAL ILLNESS.

## Re: SHOULD WE TALK ABOUT THIS?

**Gen Goldman** <GENX1999@gmail.com>

to Ava

This has nothing to do with your OCD. I'm just not doing this. I'm not having a coming out party. Nothing about me as a person has changed. I have always been this person. Who I hook up with does not define me.

## Re: SHOULD WE TALK ABOUT THIS?

**Ava Helmer** <AVA.HELMER@gmail.com>

to Gen

Well, you got me there! Congratulations. You have backed me into a PC corner. Enjoy the moral high ground.

12:32 AM EST

I HAVE THE MORAL HIGH GROUND.

How's it feel?

Eh. Less fun than drugs

When do I get to Facetime your girlfriend?

Not my girlfriend.

Excuse me.

When do I get to FaceTime your partner?

SO?

Fuck buddy?

YOU'RE HAVING SEX?!! AHHHHHHH

You're more excited than me. And the girl I'm having sex with.

Can I ask you something without it being a big deal?

What does gay sex mean?

I understand gay sex!

I don't understand lesbian sex.

Hahahaha

Google it.

I don't need to Google anymore! I have a queer best friend!

Stop labeling me.

Sorry!

**PLEDGING MY LIFE AWAY**

---

**Ava Helmer** <AVA.HELMER@gmail.com>

to Gen

Welcome to your daily Gamma Phi quiz about all things Gamma Phi! Remember, sisters are forever, and anything lower than 85% is a failing grade!

Question One: Why am I taking this quiz?

Answer: Because you don't have enough work already! We thought it would be fun to turn a social club into an extreme time commitment full of mandatory events. Including pop quizzes!

Question Two: What kind of questions can I expect?

Answer: Solely useless information that you will neither retain nor call for ever again. Topics include: history of the founding sisters, outdated dinner prayers, and boring facts about senior members who will never talk to you again.

Question Three: Aren't sororities supposed to be fun?

Answer: You have to LOOK LIKE you're having fun. There is a difference.

Question Four: Can I get my money back?

Answer: No.

Kisses and Hugs and Secret Handshakes,

A

## Re: PLEDGING MY LIFE AWAY

**Gen Goldman** <GENX1999@gmail.com>

to Ava

What's the secret handshake? I won't tell anyone.

## Re: PLEDGING MY LIFE AWAY

**Ava Helmer** <AVA.HELMER@gmail.com>

to Gen

It's very complicated. You've got to shake the other girl's hand, but instead of shaking it, you give it a light squeeze. Twice.

## Re: PLEDGING MY LIFE AWAY

---

**Gen Goldman** <GENX1999@gmail.com>

to Ava

Weird. That's also lesbian sex.

**7:12 PM PST**

We're making each other posters.

Why?

I don't know. I don't want a fucking poster.

Write that on the poster.

Can I quit yet?

You can do whatever you want.

I'M NOT A QUITTER.

I love quitting.

It feels weird that I'm essentially paying these people to hang out with me.

Did your parents not tell you I've been salaried since freshman year?

I knew it.

You were too cool to be true.

**YOU'VE BEEN CAUGHT**

---

**Gen Goldman** <GENX1999@gmail.com>

to Ava

Hypocrite.

**Re: YOU'VE BEEN CAUGHT**

---

**Ava Helmer** <AVA.HELMER@gmail.com>

to Gen

Oh, no! What did I do??? Was anyone hurt?

**Re: YOU'VE BEEN CAUGHT**

---

**Gen Goldman** <GENX1999@gmail.com>

to Ava

Just your reputation as someone who shares everything with her best friend. You thought you could follow chinatownjake98 on Instagram without me noticing?

NICE TRY! GUESS AGAIN, BITCH.

**Re: YOU'VE BEEN CAUGHT**

---

**Ava Helmer** <AVA.HELMER@gmail.com>

to Gen

How do you know that??? Do you have actual social media powers?

I only followed him because Sophia made me. She's sick of complaining about her long-distance boyfriend and wanted a distraction. I am completely ashamed.

**Re: YOU'VE BEEN CAUGHT**

---

**Gen Goldman** <GENX1999@gmail.com>

to Ava

Why are you ashamed? He followed you back.

Sophia should dump the LDR. It's destined to fail anyway.

## Re: YOU'VE BEEN CAUGHT

**Ava Helmer** <AVA.HELMER@gmail.com>

to Gen

HE FOLLOWED ME BACK??? HOW DO YOU KNOW THIS STUFF?!

## Re: YOU'VE BEEN CAUGHT

**Gen Goldman** <GENX1999@gmail.com>

to Ava

How do you NOT know this stuff?! Seriously. Your mom is better at the Internet than you.

What's your next move? And don't say unfollowing him.

## Re: YOU'VE BEEN CAUGHT

**Ava Helmer** <AVA.HELMER@gmail.com>

to Gen

Some of the girls in my house are going to his frat tonight. I guess I could go? And try to not look like a troll with social anxiety?

Did I tell you my therapist nodded at my last session? She's really opening up.

1:14 AM EST

Have a draft of my follow-up piece. Can I send it to you?

YES! Will read ASAP.

I thought you were going to the party?

I'm at the party.

AVA! You can't proofread at a fraternity.

Come on. I'm sure some of these guys are journalism majors.

I'm not sending. Go find Jake.

## FORMAL INQUIRY

---

**Ava Helmer** <AVA.HELMER@gmail.com>

to Gen

Quick question: Remember winter formal sophomore year when you told Chris R. to kiss me and then he did on our way home and I didn't realize that you could breathe through your mouth while kissing and I suffocated? Does that have to count as my first kiss?

Because I would really prefer last night to count as my first kiss. I remembered to breathe and everything.

Let me know your official opinion as the author of my future biography.

Ava

2:13 PM EST

You don't email about kissing!

You text about kissing!

A whole hour just passed with me not knowing you're a little slut!

I'm not a slut!

Slut is not bad. We are reclaiming the word "slut."

I know. But I don't think a little light kissing counts.

Ew. What is light kissing?

Minimal tongue? Lots of feelings.

Oh, boy.

I need more details but about to meet with Charlotte.

Send follow-up detailed email plz.

Tell Charlotte I say "What's good."

No.

**LOVE, LUST & BEER PONG**

---

**Ava Helmer** <AVA.HELMER@gmail.com>

to Gen

Here's the thing. Everything that happened last night was incredibly cliché bordering on boring. If it was a scene in a movie, I would have talked shit about it for being uninspired and predictable.

But that's part of what made it so special to me. It felt so . . . normal. I felt normal. Better than normal. Desired.

Gross. Gross. Scratch that from the biography.

Anyway, I showed up at ZBT around 9:30 with two girls from my pledge class, Chelsea and Emma. (Chelsea is kind of a basic bitch but she sort of knows it and doesn't care which is weirdly refreshing. Emma is British and keeps threatening to quit Gamma Phi due to all the mandatory events. Emma is my favorite.)

Side note: Why do parties start so late? What are we all trying to prove? No one does anything interesting between 7 and 10 anyway. I've started to refer to this time in my life as nightly purgatory.

Oh! I forgot to tell you what I was wearing! Black jeans and that sheer pink blouse with the gold buttons. (Don't be mad, but I wore a black tank top under it. I'm not ready to show full back yet.)

Jake was wearing a ZBT tank top and jeans. I wish I

could have stricken this part from the official record. (To be fair, all the boys wear the tank top at parties. He dresses normally when he goes to the Coffee Bean.)

As soon as we get there, I spot him talking with a freshman pledge who is also in the film school. (Crit studies, I think. Nothing impressive.) I can't tell if he's noticed me so I stare at him a few more seconds, like a complete lunatic, until Chelsea drags me away to the drink table.

Another side note: Do I have to drink to fit in? I know that this is a pathetic thing to actually ask and all after-school specials tell you: No! Of course not! But let's be real. Do I? Because I hate it.

I settle on a vodka/cranberry after Emma assures me no one roofied it. Apparently, I am being super paranoid about the whole roofying thing. I take a couple sips and pretend to know all the lyrics to some Katy Perry song as my friends dance.

Within twenty minutes, I have to pee. Because I am me and in addition to having the personality of a 65-year-old, I have a postmenopausal bladder. This is a problem for many reasons. I don't know where the bathroom is, and I can only assume said bathroom is disgusting. Even for someone without my high cleanliness standards.

Basic bitch Chelsea is already grinding cheek to cheek with some senior so I beg Emma to accompany me. She does so halfheartedly (the British, am I right?) and I lose her almost immediately. But I do find Jake. Standing alone. Waiting? Maybe? For me? Probably not.

Him: Hey.
Me: Hi! Where is your bathroom?

WHAT IS WRONG WITH ME?! Do I need to immediately appear as though I have IBS? I don't even *have* IBS. I would probably be cooler if I did have it, though, because people with IBS are so above being embarrassed for banal needs.

Him: Let me show you.

I know. This is all very cliché. But I did give you that disclaimer at the beginning.

He takes my hand (Oh my God!! Slow down!!) and leads me up the stairs to, you guessed it, his bedroom. The entire time I'm thinking: this is so lame and predictable. But also: HOLY SHIT! I'm in a boy's bedroom and . . . he is about to listen to me pee.

His room is connected to a bathroom. I have to lock like three doors because it's a shared bathroom, which is basically my worst nightmare. I quickly pop a squat and pray to the pee gods that nothing other than pee comes out. (Now would be the perfect time to actually get IBS.)

I wipe after checking the toilet paper (seemed new), wash my hands, and use my shirt to open the door, since a clean hand towel would have been too good to be true.

When I come out, I see Jake on his bed. Playing guitar.

I KNOW! I WARNED YOU! THE FOLLOWING SCENE

IS VOMIT INDUCING. DO NOT CONTINUE READING IF YOU HAVE AN AVERSION TO SINCERITY OR ARE RECENTLY PREGNANT.

Me: What are you playing?
Jake: An acoustic version of "Hotline Bling."
Me: Cool.

He laughs, which I hope means he knows how ridiculous that sounds, and then pats the bed next to him. I go over and sit down, worried because my hands are still wet from lack of a clean hand towel.

Me: Sorry. My hands are still wet from a lack of a clean hand towel.
Jake: You can wipe them on my shirt.

ARE YOU KIDDING ME? This guy is so smooth.

So now I'm wiping my hands all over his shirt, when he grabs me by the wrists, looks at me for way too long to be comfortable or sexy, and says:

Jake: I'm glad you came tonight.
Me: Same.

And then we are making out!! On a bed! It was crazy! I felt like my dad was going to walk in at any moment, which was not a great thing to think about.

His tongue was warm and beer-like. For as much as I hate beer in my mouth, I like it in his.

He tried to pull my shirt up but I stopped him. I didn't

mean to stop the whole thing, I just wanted to stop the escalation, but as soon as I did that he pulled back, kissed my hand, and said: "Let's go downstairs."

I immediately ran into Emma and got sucked into a mess about her ex-boyfriend, even though he lives in London and my could-be boyfriend was mere feet away. Jake hung around for a second but then left to hang with his friends. I went home a few minutes later while Emma ugly-cried and said "wanker" a lot. (I love this word. Am I allowed to say it?)

So that's it. That's the whole thing.

HAVE I RUINED EVERYTHING?

Please advise. And try to forget that he kissed my hand. I will do the same.

Ava

**Re: LOVE, LUST & BEER PONG**

---

**Gen Goldman** <GENX1999@gmail.com>

to Ava

Wow. I would rate this whole email NC17 (not cute unless you're 17). And we're 18 . . . so I vomited into my Moleskine.

JUST KIDDING. Everything about this seems delightfully

normal. With a touch of sap. Just remember: Jake is a typical college guy who barely knows how to take care of himself. Your self-worth should not hang in the balance of his New Balances.

What's your plan of attack? Boyfriend? Hook up? Complete avoidance? (The second one is easiest, just FYI.)

Proud of you, boo.

G

## Re: LOVE, LUST & BEER PONG

**Ava Helmer** <AVA.HELMER@gmail.com>

to Gen

Can I have a complete breakdown of the differing strategies so I can cross-reference my attraction to the energy I want to expend?

Thanks in advance and please reply in a timely manner.

## Re: LOVE, LUST & BEER PONG

**Gen Goldman** <GENX1999@gmail.com>

to Ava

The below is in no way endorsed by the FDA as an official treatment for "Horny Girl" but is highly recommended by many teens, queens, and divorcées.

**Strategy 1: Boyfriend**
Ignore him for 5 days. If he contacts you in these 5 days, you can respond but never initiate contact. Never ask questions. Remain mysterious. If he doesn't contact you, go back to his frat for a party and, this is VERY important, continue to ignore him. Talk to as many of his friends as possible while creating an illusion that you are having the best time of your young life. If he tries to talk to you, allow it, but leave early. Expect a text within 2 days. Do not agree to go over to his frat. Do not agree to do anything other than dinner. Or maybe lunch if your schedules are crazy. Wait 1 month to have sex. (DISCLAIMER: I hate this plan. It is stupid and sexist. But it also works on 95% of entitled white men.)

**Strategy 2: Hook up**
This is the most fun plan. Wait 3 days and then text him: "What are you doing?" REGARDLESS of what he responds, text: "Want to come over later?" Have sex. Or not. It's your body. Continue to hook up once a week until the spark fades or one of you falls in love and convinces the other one this is "more than a hookup." Congratulations. You have made it to the end of Strategy 1 with minimal effort. This is how you infiltrate the system

from the inside. (Disclaimer: This is by far the most dangerous strategy. It can end in heartbreak. Protect yourself.)

**Strategy 3: Complete avoidance**
Avoid the person. Completely. (Disclaimer: This might have the opposite of the desired effect and cause said person to fall in love with you. That's why the police invented restraining orders.)

There you go! Choose wisely. Or not at all.

## Re: LOVE, LUST & BEER PONG

---

**Ava Helmer** <AVA.HELMER@gmail.com>

to Gen

I have to wait five days???? That's so long! I don't think I can wait that long to do anything! Can I counter with three and a half?

**Re: LOVE, LUST & BEER PONG**

---

**Gen Goldman** <GENX1999@gmail.com>

to Ava

I see you've selected Strategy 1. May the odds be ever in your favor.

**8:42 AM PST**

I am a terrible friend!

No ur not!

Wait. Y?

Have you betrayed me?

Worse! I've forgotten about you!

Who do you think ur texting?

I mean I forgot to ask about you! How was the meeting with Charlotte?

Oh! Good.

Just good? Did she like the article?

Yeah. I think so.

You THINK so?

We mostly just hung out. Talked about journalism on a macro scale.

Am I allowed to say that's gay?

No.

## GAME RECOGNIZE GAME

**Gen Goldman** <GENX1999@gmail.com>

to Ava

I don't know how to put this politely so I will just put it: you are the craziest person I know. To be clear, I do NOT mean that as an insult. If anything, it is a testament to your extreme resilience that you're as crazy as you are and still functioning so beautifully. After years of therapy and medication . . . I'm not gonna do the whole pep talk, but you get it. You're basically an unofficial therapist.

SO! I need some semiprofessional guidance on what the fuck is going on with Molly. I can't tell if she's just "college girl acting out" or "young woman in trouble." Also, I don't know if it's even my place to say anything since I haven't known her for that long and we occasionally swap saliva so it's more complicated than if she was just a friend.

I'm not a psych major (because Emerson doesn't offer it), but the best way I can describe her behavior is manic? Not straight-up *Girl, Interrupted* but worrisome. She parties all weekend and then sleeps through class. If I don't respond right away she'll leave me a lengthy expletive-full voice mail, but by the time I call her back, she's completely over it.

Is this normal? I know no one is "normal," but is this worrisome? Her parents live nearby in Stoneham. Maybe I can suggest a visit there? Or will that seem like I'm trying to meet her parents because I'm secretly in love with her and want to lock her down in a patriarchal fashion? To be super clear, I have no intention of dating this person but care about her because I am a human being.

Gen

P.S. I can give you the full pep talk if you need it.

## Re: GAME RECOGNIZE GAME

---

**Ava Helmer** <AVA.HELMER@gmail.com>

to Gen

Hmmmm, this is a tough one. It's hard to help people who don't want help. Wanting help has always been my saving grace. I practically scream: "Help me!" from the rooftops. (If you ever bother to give me the full pep talk again, make sure you include the time I told my dad, "I need to see a doctor because something inside of me is making me sad." WHEN I WAS FOUR YEARS OLD! How has no one made a Lifetime movie about me yet?)

Is it possible that she might be a drug addict? If that's the case, you need to contact another semiprofessional because I have no experience with anything you can't be prescribed. (My Cymbalta is still making me sweaty, by the way. I've had to buy these sweat wipes for my face, but I just soak through them. It's disgusting. I'm disgusting.)

Anyway, if it's *not* a drug thing, I think you should try talking to her. Maybe open up about some of the challenges you've been facing since leaving home (I know you're perfectly independent. Make something up). Then ask if she feels the same at all. Feel free to mention the emotional mess who is your best friend. People love to open up to me about their problems. I think it's because I'm so relatable. I'm like the Sandra Bullock of mental illness.

Also, try not to hook up with her anymore. She needs a friend, not an f-buddy. Plus, promiscuity is often a side effect of mania, and you don't want to enable unhealthy behaviors.

ALREADY I HAVE GIVEN MORE PRACTICAL ADVICE THAN MY CURRENT THERAPIST WHO IS ACTUALLY LICENSED. HOW DOES ANYONE HAVE A JOB?

Keep me updated!

XO,
A

**11:14 AM EST**

I overreacted.

Fifth Harmony is not the greatest band of all time?

I never said that! I just said it was the greatest WOC girl group of our time.

You're such a liar.

Whatever.

Molly is fine. She basically laughed in my face.

Have you never heard of denial?

No. Is that in Egypt?

That joke only works out loud, you moron.

What did she say?

She said she was fine. And it was cute that I was worried about her.

And then what?

And then nothing.

You both disappeared?

No . . .

GENEVIEVE!

I tried to be a good person. I deserved some action.

Unbelievable!

🙂

## DAY 3 OF BEING TRAPPED ON THIS ISLAND

---

**Ava Helmer** <AVA.HELMER@gmail.com>

to Gen

I'm losing my mind. I can't tell up from down. I've started scratching a thin line into the foot of my bed every night to keep track of the time. My best friend is a volleyball named Willis. So I can say, "Whatchu talking about, Willis?" without Tom Hanks's attorney suing me for plagiarism.

WHY HAS HE NOT CONTACTED ME?!?!?!

Am I a bad kisser? How do I know if I am a bad kisser? I can't even kiss you now for feedback! I HATE HAVING A GAY FRIEND.

I'm lashing out. I'm so proud of you and your gayness.

I wish I was gay.

No, I don't.

I wish I was asexual.

Please delete this email. Preferably before you bother to read it.

## Re: DAY 3 OF BEING TRAPPED ON THIS ISLAND

**Gen Goldman** <GENX1999@gmail.com>

to Ava

How's your spiral? Are you enjoying it? Are there lots of twists and turns that release into a pit of blackness?

I'm going to choose to ignore your latent homophobia and instead ask you this: Why would he be liking all your Instagram photos if you're a bad kisser?

G

P.S. I'm not gay. I'm not anything. I am the darkness under your bed.

4:27 PM PST

He liked four of my photos!!!

I know.

How did you not know??

Sorority! All the girls are obligated to like each other's photos. I've never had more likes in my life! It got lost.

I still found it.

Stop gloating and tell me what to do!

DM a dick pic. 🍆

Stop saying that!

Comment on his most recent photo and go to a party at his house this weekend.

His most recent photo is of a bong.

Get out now, before it's too late.

I'm going to write: "nice."

Scratch the comment. Just go to the party.

UR better IRL.

I'm trying to be a writer!!

## NOT SO HUMBLE BRAG

---

**Gen Goldman** <GENX1999@gmail.com>

to Ava

My second article hit the newsstands this morning (not the stands but the internet). It's a hit! With our limited audience. The president of the college called over to see if she could potentially write an op-ed in response!

My editor, Kent, all but promised me a staff position

next semester. He assigned me a lengthy exposé on racist graffiti inside the Paramount Theatre. (Don't ask.)

Part of me feels like I should quit while I'm ahead and let them speak of my legend while I retire to Mexico and drink mai tais. The other part wants to keep writing until I'm the first queer female editor in chief of the *NY Times.*

Charlotte wants to take me out for a celebratory dinner. I'm a little shocked because she's mostly ignored me in class this week, but maybe she doesn't want to make it TOO obvious that I'm TA's pet.

WHAT DO I WEAR?! I HAVE NEVER HAD TO DRESS FOR PAST SUCCESS BEFORE!

Genevieve Goldman
Future Editor in Chief, *NY Times*

**1:32 PM PST**

I'm so proud of you!!!!!!

Wear your blazer.

Yeah, right.

**7:19 PM PST**

I did a bad thing . . .

Really bad.

Like accidentally launched the missiles bad.

Freaking out.

Hello?

GREAT! NOW I'M WORRIED YOU'RE DEAD TOO!

I have nothing left.

**4:27 AM EST**

What happened?

**7:52 AM EST**

Are you OK?

Ava?

Is this revenge?

**11:31 PM PST**

Where were you?

Where were YOU?

I went to the gym.

Oh, good. So your body still works.

I did a bad thing.

How bad?

Strategy 2 bad.

GIRRRRRRLLLLLLL

## IN NEED OF NEW STRATEGY

---

**Ava Helmer** <AVA.HELMER@gmail.com>
to Gen

So . . . I made an oopsie. Last night (it was really the afternoon but that sounds so pathetic) I started freaking out. I went down this weird rabbit hole where I thought maybe Jake wasn't contacting me because he didn't think I WANTED him to contact me. Also, I realized he didn't have my number! How could he contact me even if he wanted to? (I know. Twitter. Instagram. Facebook. These solutions occurred to me later.)

I was spiraling, OK? So I emailed one of the guys in my screenwriting class who is pledging ZBT and asked for Jake's number. I AM AN INSANE PERSON. Why would I do this? Because I am insane.

Exactly one hour later my friend replied with Jake's number. It is important to note that during this time I realized that I was, say it with me, insane. But I couldn't not contact him after overtly asking for his number. No way was Jake not going to hear about that.

I scraped the bottom of my brain for some viable reason other than extreme desperation to contact him and I came up with . . . Can I borrow your camera?

Before you freak out, keep in mind that I am in film school and this isn't the weirdest request. He has a Canon 5D, which I only know because he bragged about it the night we made out in his room. (Remember that night? When I was a normal college girl instead of a psychopath?)

So I spent half an hour crafting the perfect text message that seemed flirty yet casual, business-minded yet fun, and sent it off into the ether.

Nothing. For two hours. That's when I needed you most. (More on that later! Where the hell were you and why were you awake at 4 AM?)

And then . . . a reply! Not just a reply but an invitation to go over to his house so he could "teach me how to use it." Which, honestly, is a bit condescending since I am also in film school. But, to be completely fair, I had no idea how to use it. These hands were made for typing, baby!

Fast-forward three outfit changes and a mild panic attack and I'm making my way over to ZBT, alone, at night. This was dumb for many reasons including the dangerous neighborhood. When I got to the house, there were a bunch of guys hanging out in the living room. I asked if Jake was around and they asked me which Jake and then I panicked and forgot his last name. This always happens to me in moments of extreme panic. I forgot how to pronounce Veronica during one particularly stressful middle school sleepover.

One of the guys mercifully threw out a couple of Jake options and I recognized the right one. I was told he was in his room. Then the following conversation:

NICE FRAT GUY: It's up the stairs to the—
EVIL FRAT GUY: She knows where it is.
ME: *dies*

Why are boys so mean? Seriously? Why humiliate a perfectly nice girl for zero reason?

I went up the stairs, knocked on the WRONG door, and then finally found Jake's room after disappointing a nerd playing Magic: The Gathering, who looked at me like a pizza that got delivered early.

Jake, shirtless on his bed, strumming a guitar, smiled when he saw me. Not a big smile. But a smirk. Like, "I knew you'd be back." My stomach turned. I'm not sure if it was in a good way.

Long story short, he never taught me how to use the camera, but I did get felt up for the first time and now I have to shoot some sort of experimental short film or else he will think I'm obsessed with him.

WHOOPS!

A

## Re: IN NEED OF NEW STRATEGY

---

**Gen Goldman** <GENX1999@gmail.com>

to Ava

I would give this story a B-. Far too much exposition and the third act seemed rushed.

What do you mean he felt you up?! These are the kind of details I need.

I await the rewrite.

## Re: IN NEED OF NEW STRATEGY

---

**Ava Helmer** <AVA.HELMER@gmail.com>
to Gen

I'm embarrassed! The whole thing was so embarrassing! My mind kept racing and I couldn't stop thinking about his sheets. They seemed clean, but how clean could they really be? When was the last time he washed them? Would he respect me after this? What if I needed to pee? It was all overwhelming.

What are you supposed to feel when you are hooking up? Nothing? Everything?

I stopped him from going down my pants. I want to make sure we are more of a thing before that and also I want it to be on my sheets. We fell asleep around midnight, and he walked me back to my dorm in the morning. I HAD AN OUTDOOR KISS. IN THE SUNLIGHT!

I guess my big takeaway from all of this is: WHY WERE YOU AWAKE AT 4 AM? Do not think that you can deflect your whereabouts. I am a goddamn detective.

LOVE AND ANXIETY,
Ava

## Re: IN NEED OF NEW STRATEGY

**Gen Goldman** <GENX1999@gmail.com>

to Ava

Jesus, you never let anything go, do you? Even when you're in the throes of romantic passion.

I was out with Charlotte for a celebratory dinner. And drinks.

3:49 PM PST

Are you fucking kidding me?

Always.

When I check my email after my stupid induction rehearsal there better be an IN DEPTH email waiting for me.

I want details, Genevieve.

ALL the details.

🔫

## PER YOUR REQUEST

**Gen Goldman** <GENX1999@gmail.com>

to Ava

Request is putting it lightly. You should join the CIA. I hear all interrogation tactics are encouraged there. Regardless of basic human rights.

I don't know what there is to say. Other than I am hooking up with my TA.

SEE! This is how you tell a story. You lead with the fucking lede.

Now that I've hooked you, I'll take my time, since my editor, Kent, doesn't give me a word count for emails:

**YOUNG JOURNALIST SHOCKED BY INTEREST OF ELUSIVE, OLDER WOMAN**
By Genevieve Goldman
*Berkeley Beacon* Staff

BOSTON—Until last night, Genevieve Goldman, 18, had only skimmed the surface of what the Sapphic world has to offer. Upon arrival at Gaslight in the South End, her luck was about to change. Ms. Goldman, a native of Los Angeles, was meeting her Emerson College Discovering Journalism teaching assistant, Charlotte Huang, 32(????), for a celebratory dinner. Ms. Huang had invited Ms. Goldman on the pretense of mentorship, as the two had grown close over Ms. Goldman's recent investigation of a disgusting pervert who should most definitely be fired from the department of communications.

After ordering drinks, a whiskey neat for Ms. Huang and a Cherry Coke for Ms. Goldman, conversation quickly turned personal. Ms. Huang lamented a recent love affair turned sour while Ms. Goldman tried to appear cool and knowledgeable about lesbian drama (she is not). According to sociology-based social cues such as light touching and hair flipping, Ms. Huang was flirting.

Ms. Goldman, not being a complete idiot according to her closest friends and family, flirted back but didn't make any moves to advance the situation. By the end of the three-course meal (shaved beet salad, swordfish, and shared gâteau aux pommes), Ms. Goldman was reporting feelings of nausea and nerves. After a tense moment outside, Ms. Huang broke the silence with an invitation for a nightcap. At her place. This question has been documented as the singularly most successful "move" of all time.

Within 10 minutes, both women arrived at Ms. Huang's flat, sober yet elated. Within another 10 minutes, neither were sober. They were still elated. Things escalated quickly with limited talking from either party. All specific details about the goings-on were off the record, but reports suggest there were up to four goings-on. At approximately 4:27 AM, Ms. Goldman took a reprieve from her folly to answer a text from a beloved friend, who was later revealed to have made a misjudgment in Ms. Goldman's absence. Following the lack of reply from said friend, Ms. Goldman fell asleep in the arms of Ms. Huang, who clearly does Pilates or at least lifts light weights. The two separated late the next morning after a French-press coffee, courtesy of Ms. Huang's adult life.

There were unconfirmed reports of canoodling outside Ms. Huang's apartment before a red-faced Ms. Goldman made her way back to her moronic roommate and dull student life.

*To contact this reporter, please send four messenger pigeons and a Big Mac to the Piano Row dormitory at Emerson College.*

## Re: PER YOUR REQUEST

**Ava Helmer** <AVA.HELMER@gmail.com>

to Gen

WHAAAAAATTTTT!!! BUT! BUT! She's your TA! And she's ancient! And you had Cherry Coke? Please tell me that was actually just Cherry Coke the refreshing beverage and NOT Cherry Cola the code word.

Wow. Just wow. It's like you read a guidebook on how to have an outrageous college experience and then followed the steps.

At least she's not married with children. Please tell me she's not married with children.

Are you going to keep seeing her?? Is she your girlfriend? How will you act normal in class? Should you transfer to a different class? Would she get fired for this? I think she should. Not that I want her specifically to be fired, but it seems like a good policy to have in place.

This place is like Sodom and Gomorrah. Are there no rules?? No wonder that dean got hired. He could practically be Emerson's mascot.

WOW.

## Re: PER YOUR REQUEST

**Gen Goldman** <GENX1999@gmail.com>

to Ava

Hahahaha. TBD on all of your questions. Except I don't think she's married. But you never know!

5:35 PM EST

I just saw a squirrel die.

WHAT?! You killed a squirrel?

I didn't kill it!

It must have been hit by a car or something. It was freaking out and twitching.

I'm scarred for life.

Get a tattoo of the squirrel so you never forget.

Oooooo

THAT WAS A JOKE.

DO NOT GET A SQUIRREL TATTOO.

Too late

**FOR YOUR CONSIDERATION**

---

**Ava Helmer** <AVA.HELMER@gmail.com>
to Gen

SO! Crisis. Jake just texted me asking how my movie is going. Remember my movie? That pathetic invention of an excuse so I could reach out to a guy I later let feel me up? Well, guess what? That invention is about to become real. I can't have any future with Jake if our entire relationship is built on a lie. So I have to make a short film AND not look like a total idiot doing so since Jake will probably ask to see it.

Screenwriting Sophia said she would help out since she's befriended a couple of production kids and also wants to act. (All the writers want to act. All the directors want to write. The satisfaction level at this school is about zero.)

Here are some ideas. They are rough drafts just to see if I'm heading in the right direction. Please be kind.

1) A girl loses her iPhone. She has to retrace her steps to find it and in the meantime remembers how to live life without it. (But funny. Remember that it would be funny.)

2) A boy and a girl share their first kiss but neither of them enjoys it. They then proceed into a long-term relationship due to a fear of being rude. (Again, funny.)

3) A silent film from the point of view of a squirrel. (This was inspired by you. But this squirrel doesn't die. Because comedy. And also budget.)

Pick one. Pick none. Tell me to transfer to prelaw and fill out all my necessary paperwork.

## Re: FOR YOUR CONSIDERATION

**Gen Goldman** <GENX1999@gmail.com>

to Ava

Number 2! Also, you don't need to make a movie to impress some guy. But you should make a movie because you are in film school and I'm sure all the kids are doing it. Maybe start a YouTube channel! Those things can blow up!

## Re: FOR YOUR CONSIDERATION

**Ava Helmer** <AVA.HELMER@gmail.com>

to Gen

I hate YouTube. If anything, I would put it on Vimeo.

**2:32 PM EST**

Charlotte won't look at me.

Really?? I'm so sorry :(

Don't be! It's fun!

Being ignored is fun?

Oh, yeah! Now I have something to focus on in class.

How are we friends?

BRB. Knocking a pen on the floor so she can see down my shirt.

You're out of control.

## SUCCESS

---

**Gen Goldman** <GENX1999@gmail.com>

to Ava

Charlotte cornered me after class and invited me over to her place for some wine and cheese party? If this isn't the lesbian dream, I don't know what is. I'm supposed to see a show at the Comedy Studio with Molly tonight, but I'll just cancel. She bails on me all the time anyway.

I'm a bit concerned about how to act once I'm there. She probably doesn't want to make it glaringly obvious to all her friends that she is sleeping with a student. But maybe I'll linger around until everyone else leaves?

God, I love games. She is so good at games. Too bad I'm better!

LOVE AND TITS,

G

7:12 PM EST

Holy shit.

More details needed.

Molly just popped off on me for canceling.

Popped off how?

Do you know what that means?

I can infer.

She lost it. Started screaming that no one appreciates her or respects her.

What did you say?

I left.

You left???

You know I don't like to be yelled at.

And I have a fancy lesbian event to attend.

Are all of Charlotte's friends lesbians?

A girl can hope.

## SISTERHOOD OF THE TRAVELING BIMBOS

---

**Ava Helmer** <AVA.HELMER@gmail.com>

to Gen

I just spent three hours gluing sparkle Greek letters to a poster board while twenty other girls gossiped about *The Bachelorette* like the contestants are real people and not robots hired by a massive corporation to fulfill their given duties and then disappear into minor Instagram fame.

It doesn't help that I've never actually seen *The Bachelorette* . . .

I don't know. These girls take Gamma Phi so seriously. Like it's something that actually matters and not an excuse to take dumb photos and meet guys. I'm all for sisterhood in the metaphorical sense, but actual "YOU ARE MY SISTER" is creeping me out.

Am I just being a snob? Or am I trying to shove a wooden square into a small circle?

The initiation ceremony happens in two weeks. If I drop out before then I won't have to pay a full semester of dues. My mom says not to worry about the money, and my dad just keeps cracking jokes that end in Phi. (Phi ya later, etc.)

I know you are busy eating fancy cheese and trying not to go to the bathroom, but when you get a chance, I could use a good old Genevieve weigh-in.

A

**11:17 PM EST**

For my next birthday I would like a huge block of chevre, plzzz.

Go home, kid. You're drunk.

💯

But like rich drunk. This wine is $$$.

How much?

$$$$$$$

## Re: SISTERHOOD OF THE TRAVELING BIMBOS

**Gen Goldman** <GENX1999@gmail.com>

to Ava

Ava, I have read your concerns regarding BIMBOS and have some hangover thoughts. First off, the term "bimbo." Please forgo the term entirely since it is outdated and perpetuates a patriarchal vocabulary. Are you a 1940s mobster telling his wife these other women don't mean anything to him? No? Then stop saying "bimbo." Also, I doubt all of these girls are so terrible. Have you tried talking to them about other interests? Isn't one of the girls British? You can talk about Brexit!

My official, once again, hungover, Genevieve weigh-in suggests more time. Not everyone hits it off immediately. I fear that I've ruined you for other women. I am the best. We all know that. Sometimes you have to settle.

I CAN HEAR THE CREAKS IN THE FLOOR TWO STORIES ABOVE ME. IF MY HEAD EXPLODES, PLEASE KEEP MY BRAIN GOOP FOR SCIENCE.

Ow. Ow. Ow.

G

**12:43 PM PST**

Have contacted the CDC. They are scheduling body pickup.

The CDC??? You think I have a disease?

They were just the first government agency to answer the phone.

How are you feeling?

Is death a feeling?

Drink Gatorade and don't think this gets you out of a full disclosure of last night's event.

Stop pushing Gatorade on me.

Sorry, I signed a brand deal.

♥

## GENDER IS OVER (IF YOU WANT IT)

**Gen Goldman** <GENX1999@gmail.com>

to Ava

Charlotte might be my soul mate if I believed in soul mates and was interested in a monogamous relationship. Her friends, mostly other grad students from every college in New England, are cool and smart and talk to me like I'm a person even though I just became one like a month ago.

They are not all lesbians, but even the token cis straight guy had a feminine quality and BEAUTIFUL hair. It started out very casual, but by midnight everyone was red wine drunk and smoking from a bong shaped like an elephant Charlotte bought in India. I abstained from the bong because I needed my wits about me. This poetry

TA from Amherst clearly had her eyes on my girl as well. By the end of the party it became a stand-off for her affection, but GUESS WHAT? College kids don't need to sleep! Cathleen lost stamina at 2 AM and went home, leaving me with Charlotte, who was too wasted to do anything other than stroke my hair and tell me all the awards I will win one day. It was the most satisfying interaction of my life. (Don't worry, we still fornicated in the morning.)

She told me this morning that her friend is coming into town tomorrow so we'll have to cool it for a week or two. What kind of person crashes for a week or two? (I know that's what you are thinking.) Apparently, Charlotte hosts people all the time. She likes to feed off different creative energy.

I don't care, though. It's not like we're dating. We're exploring. And now I can explore other people ;)

GG

## Re: GENDER IS OVER (IF YOU WANT IT)

---

**Ava Helmer** <AVA.HELMER@gmail.com>

to Gen

Feeding off their energy??? Really?? This whole email seemed like a pamphlet from one of those spiritual people at the airport.

I'm happy for you? I don't understand you, but I'm happy for you.

Now go explore with people your own age.

**10:24 AM EST**

My professor has a booger.

Ewwwww. Tell him.

I keep gesturing to my nose but this guy is not picking up what I'm putting out.

Has everyone noticed?

I can only assume.

How are you texting in class?

It's connected to my computer.

😈

**7:16 PM PST**

Jake asked me to come over.

No.

I just write back no???

Write back "No. Next idea, please."

YOU ARE SO GOOD.

Please hold.

He's typing . . .

"Dinner?"

I'm a fucking genius. People should pay me to tell them what to do.

What should I wear???

I have no idea.

## ELIZABETH TAYLOR AND RICHARD BURTON

---

**Ava Helmer** <AVA.HELMER@gmail.com>

to Gen

Can you tell that I go to film school???

Let me set the scene.

INT. EL CHOLO—NIGHT

Two nervous college students make small talk about films only one of them has seen. The food arrives. AVA, 18, doesn't really like hers but pretends to.

JAKE
So when are you shooting the big movie?

AVA chokes on a tortilla chip. It's not cute.

AVA
Within the next few weeks. Still finalizing some stuff. Like the crew and location and script.

JAKE
Nice. Sweet. Cool. Who is playing the main guy?

AVA
Oh, we are also still finalizing the actors.

JAKE
I act, you know.

AVA almost eats another tortilla chip but stops herself.

AVA

Anything I would have seen? Like a guest star on *Law & Order*?

YOU GET IT! I'm not very good at dating, and Jake wants to be in my movie! EEP!

Do you think this is a good idea? Bad idea? Neutral?

Part of me feels like this is the most obvious, cliché way for us to fall in love until one of us goes on a semester abroad. The other part of me feels like this is my project and I am really worried about doing it correctly and when I am worried I tend to be my "worst self" and maybe he will think I am a bitch even though I am just bossy and know what I want. (Thank you for helping me reclaim the word.)

I didn't know how to respond, so I told him he would have to audition. He laughed at this, thinking it was some sort of sexy innuendo even though I was being serious. I laughed back and then tried his chili margarita because some guy on Alvarado Street made him a fake ID last semester.

He asked me to go back to his room after, but I played hard to get because my stomach hurt and because I was afraid. I don't know if my stomach hurting was psychosomatic or a result of the food. Either way, I think our next "date" shouldn't involve a meal. If there even is a next date. Apparently, I have to hold an audition first!

SEND HELP, LOVE, AND ADVICE.

A

## Re: ELIZABETH TAYLOR AND RICHARD BURTON

---

**Gen Goldman** <GENX1999@gmail.com>

to Ava

Hmmmm. Interesting. This guy is aggressive, for sure. I admire the confidence but also find it off-putting from a straight white male. I think if you have any hesitation about it then you shouldn't do it. This is your first short and that's stressful enough. You don't want to have to worry about some guy's feelings on set.

That said, all I want to do is write with Charlotte for the rest of my life, so what do I know?

P.S. Did you see on Instagram that Tracy got a tattoo? Of a POT LEAF???? She made us stop watching *Minority Report* because it was rated R. COLLEGE CHANGES PEOPLE!

## Re: ELIZABETH TAYLOR AND RICHARD BURTON

**Ava Helmer** <AVA.HELMER@gmail.com>

to Gen

That was actually me. And it was rated PG-13. But I still thought I was too young to properly ingest the content.

**8:06 PM EST**

Kent just called himself my editor. Out loud.

hahahahaha

It's like he can hear us.

I wouldn't be surprised. He's an investigative journalist.

Change my name in your contacts.

## THERE ARE THREE TYPES OF PEOPLE IN THIS WORLD

**Gen Goldman** <GENX1999@gmail.com>

to Ava

And they all go to journalism school. Allow me to explain. As a rough draft of my future exposé titled "There Are Three Types of People In This World: And They All Go to Journalism School." (We are paid by the word.)

The aforementioned Kent, my editor, falls under "Watergate devotees." This paranoid group of young go-getters thinks they are always one article away from taking down the U.S. government. Watergate was their first coming and Edward Snowden is their messiah.

The second type of "journalist" is "Carrie Bradshaw meets Dan Savage." They think their own lives are newsworthy enough to warrant a story and are unable to remain "objective." Very fun at parties, awful in class.

Finally, we arrive at "If Hunter S. Thompson was in *Almost Famous*." Write drunk, edit sober. Except they're never sober. For every groundbreaking piece there are 15 paragraphs of incoherent LSD-fueled trash.

Where do I fall, you might ask? I don't subscribe to labels. Unless I'm labeling other people.

G

**Re: THERE ARE THREE TYPES OF PEOPLE IN THIS WORLD**

---

**Ava Helmer** <AVA.HELMER@gmail.com>

to Gen

I would peg you as a "Watergate devotee" with a healthy dose of cynicism.

I haven't quite pegged the three different types of

screenwriters, but there seems to be a real divide among the film majors.

Production major: Making movies since childhood. Already knows how to use a camera. Wants to specialize in directing. Snob.

Screenwriting major: Loves movies. Horrible at technical aspects of filmmaking such as "the line" and lighting. Not popular in high school. Most likely to make money.*

Critical studies major: Wanted to be a production major but didn't get in. (See above for personality type.)

Animation major: Mysterious.

*I, however, won't ever make any money because my script for the short is ATROCIOUS! How did I get into this school? Did they even read my application? I must have been some sort of mailing error they were too embarrassed to fix.

4:32 PM PST

Remember that time you ghostwrote a note for me and then Brett Collins and I hooked up in your car as a result?

Yes . . .

PROOF YOU ARE A GREAT WRITER.

You said his saliva tasted like soy sauce.

That's on him. Not you.

UR a ★.

**8:15 PM PST**

Uh-oh.

SpaghettiOs!

Why are all of your references not of this time??

Old soul.

What's up?

Molly wants me to go to the party with her . . .

Have you talked since the big blowout?

Nope.

Do you want to go?

Nope.

So you're gonna . . .

Go. Obviously. It's a party.

MAKE GOOD DECISIONS.

## AWKWARD TURTLE

**Gen Goldman** <GENX1999@gmail.com>

to Ava

So . . . last night happened. And it was fucking weird.

I went to that party with Molly around 10 (because parties start at 10), and it was fine but nothing special. I feel like art students are performing instead of living. And it's not that fun to talk to a caricature of a human being. If I found out that I was actually talking to an alien PRETENDING to be a human, sign me up. An actual human who can't relate to emotion and empathy? No, thanks.

Anyway, around 1, I wanted to bail, and Molly insisted on coming with me (even though she ignored me all night). She was hungry and dragged me to this pizza place called New York Pizza. Hilarious. After making a scene because they didn't carry pineapples (???), she calmed down enough to sit on a bench outside and wait for me to bring her the food, which I also had to pay for. I stayed inside waiting for our calzones, which take FOREVER. By the time they were finally ready, I walked outside into a full-blown shit storm. Charlotte was standing there with her friend from out of town, this stunning Nigerian woman, Essie, while Molly screamed at her.

Yes, my friend/hookup, Molly, was yelling at my TA/lover, Charlotte. In front of a beautiful, worldly woman. Do you remember Molly's torturous ex, Charlie?

Charlie = Charlotte and Charlotte = Charlie.

YEP!

And apparently things did not end well between them. Molly was shouting something about dignity when I strolled up, in shock. But Charlotte remained cool, barely looking my way, not giving anything away. She let Molly go on for a bit until she tired herself out. (FYI, this is a great tactic to use when someone is shouting at you.) Essie even pulled out her phone at one point before introducing herself to me very casually while Molly screamed, "I am not a toy!"

Eventually, Molly stopped to catch her breath and Charlotte stroked her hair, somehow making her feel taken care of and stupid for acting out. Within a moment both women were gone, and Molly was stuffing her face with a calzone.

Like . . . what do I do now??? Do I tell Molly I'm sleeping with Charlotte? (I'm thinking: NO.) Do I reach out to Charlotte to apologize for Molly's behavior? Or do I just do nothing at all and wait for everything to die down? (Seems like a solid plan.)

I think I need to put the kibosh on the whole Molly situation. This girl is unstable and not in a manic-pixie-dream-girl-good-times way.

HOW WAS YOUR NIGHT?

G

## Re: AWKWARD TURTLE

---

**Ava Helmer** <AVA.HELMER@gmail.com>

to Gen

Whoa. This Charlotte gets around. Is she dating that Essie girl too? I don't understand your life.

I know this is unlike me, but I think you're right. No plan is the best plan. Other than staying away from Molly. And maybe eating more vegetables.

My night was fine. Hung out at the house and tried to feel like "one of the girls." I don't know. My entire involvement at Gamma Phi feels forced. There is ANOTHER football game this weekend that we are encouraged (expected) to attend. I think I might just go home instead. I wonder how many different "family birthday parties" I'll have to attend this year to get out of things. I might need to transition to funerals at some point . . .

OK. Off to go audition Jake. I told him he had to do a chemistry read with Sophia before I could hand him the part. Here's hoping the poorly written sides won't make him change his mind!

**Re: AWKWARD TURTLE**

---

**Gen Goldman** <GENX1999@gmail.com>

to Ava

Why are you auditioning Jake??? I thought we decided you don't need no man???

4:32 PM PST

I'm auditioning Jake because I am dumb and weak.

Also he is so cute and I have nothing and no one.

Cool. Just needed clarification.

## AND THE OSCAR GOES TO...

---

**Ava Helmer** <AVA.HELMER@gmail.com>

to Gen

Another white person!

But for real, Sophia is SO good. I had no idea. I basically just cast her in an attempt to strengthen our friendship and get free access to gear. But the girl has chops. Jake was pretty good too. He ad-libbed some lines, which I didn't LOVE, but then again, art is about collaboration yada yada. (I want to write movies alone in my room.)

*I'M MAKING A FILM!!!

**I'm making a short film!!

I'm making a student film.

**11:47 PM EST**

Hypothetically, can I get fired for hooking up with my editor?

Kent???? Your editor, Kent????

NO!

Any editor.

Or would only the editor get fired and I can sue for sexual harassment?

Is this really just a hypothetical?

Yep.

I'll ask my dad.

👌

## SUPERMAN VS LEX LUTHOR

**Gen Goldman** <GENX1999@gmail.com>

to Ava

I have a nemesis. Which is actually great because I always thought you weren't an interesting person until at least a few people hated you.

His name is Alex. He's the only other freshman who has any real shot of getting a news staff position next semester. He hasn't written anything groundbreaking at Emerson, but he won a big-time national award for his high school paper last year. An exposé on gendered elementary school bathrooms. He's trans BTW. Which is the equivalent of having a private plane at Emerson and probably nowhere else. (I'm not outing him, for the record. It's public knowledge.)

Am I upset that my nemesis is a socially conscious, dapper prodigy? You bet! But his cleverly worded group emails aren't fooling me. Behind his Pride-stickered laptop is a conniving jerk who is only out for himself. He's already spreading rumors that I "got lucky" with my dean story and I have yet to prove myself as an actual journalist.

Too bad no one ever told him that rage is my secret weapon!

"That's my secret, Cap. I'm always angry."

BITCHES AND HOS,

G

**Re: SUPERMAN VS LEX LUTHOR**

---

**Ava Helmer** <AVA.HELMER@gmail.com>

to Gen

OK. Lots to process here. How do you know he is spreading rumors? And isn't it better to not engage? Maybe just put your head down and do the work!

Sigh. Even as I am writing this, I know it is a waste of time. I'm going to turn on the news and see that you got involved in some lightsaber battle with *Out* magazine's student of the year.

The worst part is this super-unhealthy rivalry will probably make you a better journalist.

*"Follow your heart but take your brain with you."*
—A top 10 funny quote according to Google search

Ava

**Re: SUPERMAN VS LEX LUTHOR**

---

**Gen Goldman** <GENX1999@gmail.com>

to Ava

Let's end every email with a ridiculous quote! Mine will all be from the Marvel Cinematic Universe!

Rumor has it that Alex made a few biting remarks at a Beacon party last weekend and he actively rolled his eyes at me this morning in a meeting. Plus, he REFUSES to follow me back on Twitter. And his Instagram is private. WHAT ARE YOU HIDING, ALEX?!

I'm going to take this asshole down. Even if I have to kiss Kent's "Editor" butt outside of business hours, I'll put on ChapStick and get to it! Office Gen: pretty good time. Party Gen: unstoppable.

Eat shit. (Not you.)

*"Genius, Billionaire, Playboy, Philanthropist."*
—Genevieve Goldman

**8:36 PM PST**

Sophia broke up with her boyfriend!

Called it.

She's being eerily calm about it.

She didn't like that guy.

???

How would you know that?

I assume no one likes anyone until uve been married for like 20 years.

According to that logic, your parents must like each other . . .

HOLY SHIT! I'd completely forgotten I have parents!

😈

My mom won't stop texting me about "Jane the Virgin."

Ruth!! What a softie!

Have you really not called your parents??

No comment.

## CHRISTIAN BALE VS THE DP

---

**Ava Helmer** <AVA.HELMER@gmail.com>

to Gen

Hate to steal your thunder, but you're no longer the only person with a nemesis. Although, in my case, as you can see from the subject line, both the antagonist and the protagonist are heavily flawed.

Who is the incompetent cinematographer to my grisly Christian Bale (tortured/talented)? Why, it's none other than my obnoxious teen therapist, Lily. Finally found out her first name! And it's adorable, which makes it hard to scream in a believably angry way.

After weeks of not talking, other than to ask me to repeat myself, only for her to NOT write anything down, Dr. Lily decides to make an announcement. Apparently, I'm incredibly defensive. Defensive to what? Her soft chewing of hard candy? (Seriously, we're talking three different Life Savers in the course of one hour.)

I wasn't even sure that this woman was capable of audible speech and suddenly she's accusing me of building walls and refusing to see anything outside of my own "self-diagnosis." She had the audacity to ask me why I even come to therapy if I already have everything figured out and under control. I HAVE NOTHING FIGURED OUT AND EVERYTHING IS OUT OF CONTROL. Anyone who knows me knows this. Plus, I have to go the therapy or my parents will pull me out of school. That was the deal.

I tried to explain this to her, calmly, and she said, and I quote, “Why are you so angry?” WELL, NOW I’M REALLY ANGRY. Nothing pisses me off more than someone telling me I’m pissed off. (I have to assume this is an innate biological reaction, because how else would anyone respond to such infuriating commentary?)

The rest of the session was an angry blur. But I tried to explain my point of view.

1) I’m not defensive, I’m just filling the time with my own observations because she never says anything.

2) I’m more well versed in my particular brand of illness because I have been living with it for 14 years and she just met me.

3) I am very self-aware and do not find myself to be abnormally defensive.

Instead of engaging me in a conversation about her brand-new interpretation of me, she clammed up and leaned her head to one side. Do you know what’s the most effective way to make someone sound defensive? Force her to talk, for 20 minutes, about how she’s totally NOT defensive.

She is an evil genius. And I will destroy her.

I just want to go back to Dr. Miles and her comfy couch in Santa Monica. Maybe she can do Skype sessions. Or my parents will let me bring my car. A bunch of other freshmen have cars. I'm sure I can find three hours in the middle of the week to drive across the city and have a nice familiar face tell me that I'm making great progress.

*"I hate therapy."*—Ava Helmer, 2017

## Re: CHRISTIAN BALE VS THE DP

---

**Gen Goldman** <GENX1999@gmail.com>

to Ava

I appreciate your commitment to ending every email with a quote, but I have to call technicality on quoting yourself. If you became a meme or something, then MAYBE you could send said meme back to me, but until you go viral, please refer to outside sources.

What were you guys talking about when all of this happened?

*"Whatever happens tomorrow, you must promise me one thing. That you will stay who you are. Not a perfect soldier, but a good [wo]man."*—Stanley Tucci

G

**Re: CHRISTIAN BALE VS THE DP**

**Ava Helmer** <AVA.HELMER@gmail.com>
to Gen

We were talking about this kid in my writing class, Ben, who always critiques me unnecessarily. I can handle notes, but this guy goes after me, every time. And then, yesterday, he told me not to get defensive. Which obviously sparked a new word in Dr. Lily and she held on to it for dear life.

You don't think I'm defensive, do you?

**Re: CHRISTIAN BALE VS THE DP**

**Gen Goldman** <GENX1999@gmail.com>
to Ava

How about them Yankees? Gonna be a great year.

**Re: CHRISTIAN BALE VS THE DP**

**Ava Helmer** <AVA.HELMER@gmail.com>
to Gen

Genevieve!

## Re: CHRISTIAN BALE VS THE DP

---

**Gen Goldman** <GENX1999@gmail.com>

to Ava

OK. OK. Are you defensive? Yes. But everyone is defensive. And I think it's a bit different for you because you do a lot of work of explaining your own behavior and thoughts to yourself so it's extra hard to hear an outsider's point of view and/or someone who spends no time considering her own actions (aka someone like me).

ALSO, this woman sees you as highly functioning. She doesn't necessarily understand where you are coming from and the work you've had to do to get to this place. (Like me.)

So in conclusion, maybe you are defensive. But that doesn't mean you will always be defensive. If anyone knows how to change for the better, it's you. Remember when you used to shower three times a day? What are you down to now??

Life is a journey. Namaste.

## Re: CHRISTIAN BALE VS THE DP

**Ava Helmer** <AVA.HELMER@gmail.com>
to Gen

I'm down to one shower and a foot wash.

I see your point. But I still hate her and hard candies.

**2:56 PM PST**

I just fell down in front of a large group of people.

Fell down how?

Tripped or touched ground?

Full ground.

Send pic.

I stood back up!

So ur fine ;)

I hope one day something truly embarrassing happens to you and you are forced to understand my daily struggle.

You can't be embarrassed if you don't get embarrassed.

I hate you.

RIP. love u 2

**3:12 PM EST**

Charlotte wants to see me in her office.

That's good!

- Home is good.
- Office is bad.
- The drawbacks of banging your teacher.
- #slutlife

## HOT CO-ED NEWSLETTER

---

**Gen Goldman** <GENX1999@gmail.com>

to Ava

Turns out we had to meet in her office because her house was occupied. For a second, I thought she wanted to talk about my latest paper, because she handed it to me, but then I realized we just hadn't closed the door yet and one of her colleagues was walking by. But then the door closed and work was over for the day!

Get it? We had sex in her office!

Very exciting and uncomfortable. I think people do stuff on a bed for a reason, but it was a real rush. Definitely something for the spank bank.

Afterward, I tried to talk to her about the whole Molly episode, but she brushed it off. Apparently, they were barely together and Molly just likes drama. I asked her if she thought I should stay friends with her, and Charlotte said she didn't care either way. I didn't bother to share that Molly and I have hooked up because the whole thing seemed so childish in the fluorescent glow of her cramped shared office.

Molly hasn't reached out anyway, so I think it's a nonissue.

If it wasn't clear, I feel very accomplished and cool.

G

## Re: HOT CO-ED NEWSLETTER

**Ava Helmer** <AVA.HELMER@gmail.com>

to Gen

You had sex in her office??? What is wrong with this person?? Is she actively trying to get fired??

Didn't you write an entire exposé about a teacher's inappropriate behavior with his students? Why is this OK? Because it's a female teacher??

I really feel like you need to be careful. Weekends, whatever. I'm not your mother. Or my mother. But stop flirting with danger. It's getting ridiculous.

## Re: HOT CO-ED NEWSLETTER

**Gen Goldman** <GENX1999@gmail.com>

to Ava

Thank you for the concern, but you're freaking out over nothing. I'm trying to get that sleazy dean fired because of sexual HARASSMENT. What happened today was completely consensual and THAT is why it is different.

You make me not want to tell you stuff when you react like this.

## Re: HOT CO-ED NEWSLETTER

**Ava Helmer** <AVA.HELMER@gmail.com>

to Gen

Don't do that. Don't make it seem like I have to agree with everything you do in order to stay in your life. That's not what friends are for. If you want a yes-woman, make a lot of money and buy one.

**Re: HOT CO-ED NEWSLETTER**

---

**Gen Goldman** <GENX1999@gmail.com>

to Ava

It's possible to disagree with someone without sounding like a judgy, condescending asshole.

I'm not a moron. I'm not going to get kicked out of school. Even if we got caught, so what? It's not like she's my professor and I'm blowing her to get an A. She's not even in charge of my grade!

You need to chill out and grow up.

**8:14AM EST**

**9:32AM PST**

**#TBT**

---

**Gen Goldman** <GENX1999@gmail.com>

to Ava

Can I post that photo of you with the braces and the American flag tankini? With the caption "In orthodonture we trust"?

Too late. I already posted.

**Re: #TBT**

---

**Ava Helmer** <AVA.HELMER@gmail.com>

to Gen

I'm assuming this is your social media olive branch? Mass humiliation?

**Re: #TBT**

---

**Gen Goldman** <GENX1999@gmail.com>

to Ava

Jake liked it. Which means he's looking at your tagged photos on Instagram . . .

**Re: #TBT**

---

**Ava Helmer** <AVA.HELMER@gmail.com>

to Gen

Shut up! I like him so much. I hope he can't tell.

7:29 PM EST

Nemesis alert!

You ran into Dr. Lily?

MY nemesis!

Alex and I were in Emerson's gender-neutral bathroom at the same time and he said NOTHING!

He ignored you after you said hi?

I didn't say hi!

Then you ignored him!

No!

I was already at the sink when he came up. The person to join the sink last has to say hello.

What weird knockoff Miss Manners book did your mom buy you?

My mom doesn't buy books. You know that.

I think maybe you are being an instigator in this rivalry.

You come at the king, you BEST not miss.

I'm just glad you washed your hands.

**SEX?**

---

**Ave Helmer** <AVA.HELMER@gmail.com>

to Gen

Did I do it? Did I not do it? I guess you'll have to watch (read) to find out:

TITLE CARD: 7 HOURS EARLIER

I hold an informal table read in my dorm's common area with Jake, Sophia, Emma, and our DP, Curtis. (Emma is a theater major and plays the one other role.) Jake tried to sit next to me but I told him to sit next to Sophia so they could play off each other. He then sat VERY close to Sophia, which, if we're being honest, made me uncomfortable. Also, single Sophia is a lot more flirtatious than long-distance-relationship Sophia. I think I saw her touch his leg. Leg is a bold move!

I haven't given Sophia all the dirty details about me and Jake, but she knows I like him and that we have been intimate (exactly two times and with one semifancy dinner). I doubt she would really make a pass at him, but that's probably what Jennifer Aniston thought before Angelina ruined her life (and then Brad's).

In better news, the reading went really well! Curtis, a junior who barely speaks, guffawed at a few of the lines, and Emma complimented me on my "clever dialogue." I still need to make a few changes, mostly due to production concerns, but I think it's shaping up! "Good

Manners" should have a wide theatrical release in no time!

I think we have to shoot the final scene at my parents' house, BTW. So . . . there's that. And the idea of Jake meeting my dad, who will either ignore him completely or try to show off with actual magic tricks. Can't wait!

THE END

Just kidding! After the reading, Jake asked me what I was doing, and I replied, "Why don't you tell me?" because I have seen too many cheesy films and like to make it hard for myself to fall asleep when there are so many mortifying moments to replay in my mind.

Luckily for me, he ignored my rom-com come-on and invited me over to his room to watch *When Harry Met Sally.* YEP! He invited me over to see one of my favorite movies of all time. If that's not true love . . .

CUT TO:

Jake's room. The movie is playing. His arm is around me. I lean in and whisper, "Do you think Sophia's pretty?"

I'M THE WORST. I know. BUT. It was almost worth it because:

JAKE: Not as pretty as you.

A few minutes later, I saw my first penis.

END SCENE.

10:42 AM EST

What the actual fuck.

We didn't fuck! I thought I made that clear!

What did you do???

At this point I'm gonna assume he put it in your ear if ur not more specific.

Do people do that???

Ava. Cut the bullshit.

OK. Sorry. It's embarrassing.

Y? Was it crooked?

Gross! No!

There is nothing gross about that. All bodies are beautiful.

Spare me right now. I'm recovering from a hand job.

WHAT!!! People still give hand jobs in the year of our Lord 2017???

I thought so!! Was I not supposed to do that??

Did he tell you to stop?

No!

Then more power to you.

I feel weird and also excited.

Same.

******CONGRATULATIONS******

---

**Gen Goldman** <GENX1999@gmail.com>

to Ava

On seeing a penis! So proud of you, bb.

**Re: ****CONGRATULATIONS******

**Ava Helmer** <AVA.HELMER@gmail.com>

to Gen

Thank you??? The rush is over and now the anxiety is settling in like a familiar flu.

Did I move too quickly?? Is he going to lose all interest and respect for me?

I know this is completely backward and sexist, but the media has ingrained this way of thinking in my brain and I am not stronger than the media.

It's been 12 hours since I saw him, and no contact. I've started imagining that he's run off to Paris with Sophia and Curtis. (Curtis is there to document the trip for later Instagram posts. And to carry the luggage.)

HELP!

**Re: ****CONGRATULATIONS******

**Gen Goldman** <GENX1999@gmail.com>

to Ava

OK. Calm down. It's been 12 hours. And I am saying that in a casual it's-only-been-12-hours voice and not in an IT'S-BEEN-12-WHOLE-HOURS!-THE-MISSING-PERSON-MUST-BE-DEAD! voice.

I understand the anxiety. You're facing a whole new world of genitals and feelings. But from everything you've told me, this guy Jake likes you. And he doesn't seem to have that much going on.

I'm sure he's just trying to play it cool. Or he might still be sleeping. Some people sleep past 8:30 AM.

Also, this is one dumb guy in one dumb college. (No offense. But it's not even ranked that high.) You have lived without him for 18 years. You can live without him for 18 more.

And then maybe you'll run into each other at a supermarket, rekindle the flame, and leave your current spouses for a rocky second marriage!

Isn't life exciting???

G

**5:12 PM PST**

USC is the #1 film school in the country.

Emerson is the #1 gay school in the country.

Any contact from you know who?

No. I'm freaking.

Emma wants me to go out on the row with

her tonight. But what if Jake thinks I'm stalking him?

Go everywhere but his house.

I have to go to his house! I'm stalking him!

I can't help you.

## NOT ALL CONSPIRACIES ARE THEORIES

**Gen Goldman** <GENX1999@gmail.com>

to Ava

It's 3 AM. Do you know where your children are?

I'm in my room, a little high, and thinking about Edward Snowden. I know! I've said it before. But that man is a hero. I think I need to find him and thank him with my body. I wonder if he gets a lot of ass in Russia, or if no one cares because the Russian government is obviously corrupt so it's like "big whoop."

Do you think he has met Putin? Do you think anyone has really met Putin? Is he the kind of guy you can really *know*?

My roommate is snoring. This is a new development. I don't like it.

What if I am the next Edward Snowden? I guess I would have to infiltrate the NSA for a few years. But I'd be willing to go undercover for the sake of our great nation.

I want to be a hero, Ava. Or really rich. I think it's easy to make yourself a hero when you can pay for it.

I know you fantasize about accepting your Oscar and thanking your parents after falling on the steps to the podium, but I fantasize about meeting a source in a parking garage and putting my entire family at risk.

I WANT TO BE GREAT, AVA! I WANT TO WRITE THINGS THAT CHANGE THE WORLD AND WALK INTO ROOMS FULL OF PEOPLE WHO FEAR ME!

I will have a legacy without having a stretched-out vagina from childbirth!!

POWER TO THE FOURTH ESTATE!

## Re: NOT ALL CONSPIRACIES ARE THEORIES

**Gen Goldman** <GENX1999@gmail.com>
to Ava

WOW! I was so high last night hahahahahhha.

**7:12 AM PST**

Texting you from inside enemy territory.

Russia???

What? No!

Did you read my email?

Not yet. I just woke up . . .

Did something bad happen??

Yes, to the American people.

I got high and watched "Citizenfour" twice.

Again???

Yep! Where are you?

Jake's room.

WTF?!

I know! I'm freaking out!

This is my first sleepover since 7th grade when I made my mom pick me up from Rachel's house because the sheets were dirty.

Thinking about your childhood makes me sad.

How did you handle frat boy sheets?

Alcohol and breathing exercises.

ALCOHOL???

You hate alcohol!

Very much.

I need full details.

Too hard to type. His body is crushing my arm.

Kinky.

## ABOUT LAST NIGHT

**Ava Helmer** <AVA.HELMER@gmail.com>
to Gen

It was an evening a lot like most. Moderate Southern California air that still made me feel cold. Laughter and off-color jokes in the air. Emma picked me up at my dorm and we walked over to the row together. All the Gamma Phi pledges were going to the 9-0 but Emma wanted a break from all of the girls we are paying to be friends with. She's been flirting with some Lambda Chi guy and wanted a second opinion. Apparently, her ex was a complete nightmare but no one bothered to tell her.

Pat, her guy, wasn't *quite* a nightmare, but he was nightmare adjacent. He made us do shots upon entry and then tried to hand me off to one of his friends so Emma would make out with him in the corner. It was actually really sweet. They would make out for a few minutes and then she would ask if I was OK, then they would make out for a few more minutes and she'd ask if I was OK. Carl, the guy I was handed off to, refused to look me in the eye and spent our precious time together checking out other girls. Within 20 minutes, I was exhausted and ready to go home. I thought about meeting the other pledges at the bar but decided not every night of my young college life has to be fun.

I tapped Emma on the bare shoulder a few times and told her I forgot to plug my computer in. YEP! That was my excuse. They don't call me one-shot Helmer for nothing! Luckily Emma was in such a snog-fog (her word, not mine) that she didn't question it.

I started the long walk of lame home only to hear my name shouted from the rooftops. Seriously. The guys at ZBT put lawn chairs on their roof, and Jake was standing up screaming at me.

This was both the most mortifying and thrilling moment of my entire life. And I am including the time I won my dad a day with Cal Ripken Jr. and had to recite my winning essay in front of the other participants.

I had to yell back at him to stop, only for him to scream, "MEET ME IN MY ROOM."

Looks like my walk of lame was quickly becoming a walk of shame before I even took any of my clothes off.

I arrived at his room a good TEN MINUTES before him. Apparently roof access is treacherous. When he finally arrived, I was in full-blown panic attack mode. But then he saw me and whistled and I relaxed. Jake, drunk, is very fun. Is that bad to say? He's goofy and fun and makes it easy for me to say whatever I want without feeling like there will be dramatic repercussions. We also started kissing very quickly, which was nice. You know how I feel about pretense.

Have I always fantasized about losing my virginity to a wasted sophomore in the middle of a party? Nope! But luckily he fell asleep before that happened! I don't want to diagnose him with ED because I'm not a doctor, but there were definitely symptoms. Such as his erection having a dysfunction.

It was probably a one-time alcohol thing . . .

BUT! What if alcohol isn't the problem? And I'm the problem?? I certainly didn't look good enough last night to keep Creepy Carl's interest. Maybe I just wasn't doing it for him. I mean, there are plenty of people I'm not attracted to (most people). What if Jake isn't attracted to me at all, and I've just been making a fool of myself the entire time? He didn't try any funny business in the morning either! Although he was hungover and his roommate had crawled into bed sometime when we were already asleep. He offered to walk me to my dorm, but I declined because I continuously cock-block myself.

In conclusion, how can you want to fuck Edward Snowden? I thought you were gay now.

## Re: ABOUT LAST NIGHT

---

**Gen Goldman** <GENX1999@gmail.com>

to Ava

I have so many angry thoughts I don't know which one to e-shout at you first! But since I am selfish, I guess I will start with the one about me!

I am perfectly within my queer rights to want to fuck

Edward Snowden. Sexuality is like a river, and sometimes it bends right into America's greatest hero.

Also, have you heard of the colloquial term "BISEXUAL"? Stop trying to make me in your heteronormative image!

Back to my other trigger warning. YOU ARE NOT THE PROBLEM. Never blame yourself for the physical failings of a man. Their infrastructure is designed for malfunction.

Do you think men ever sit at home and think about how THEY'RE THE PROBLEM?? No way. So don't waste your thoughts either.

Also, and I hate myself for asking, but I feel like you've conditioned me: Have you guys had any sort of talk? About what you are? Do you think you want to have sex if you haven't DTR? I'm not saying you should marry the guy (please don't marry the guy), but it might be worth having a check-in to make sure you're on the same page.

I can talk to him too if you want. I am very good at making empty threats of violence seem real.

**Re: ABOUT LAST NIGHT**

---

**Ava Helmer** <AVA.HELMER@gmail.com>

to Gen

I looked up "bisexuality" and some leading scientists have inconclusive evidence that it might be real.

(JK JK OMG JUST KIDDING)

Thank you for saying that thing about DTR. I've wanted to bring it up so many times but I don't know how and I don't want to seem clingy.*

*I can't believe how enduring one comment from one summer camp boyfriend can be. (I was 11 years old, Kyle! Of course I was clingy!)

What should I say? How should I say it? WHEN should I say it?

I hate feeling like I am never going to hear from him ever again each time we say goodbye. I know this can't be true, mostly because he is in my movie, but still. I don't trust that he won't disappear just like every other confidant other than you.

Please include specific instructions, as always.

## Re: ABOUT LAST NIGHT

---

**Gen Goldman** <GENX1999@gmail.com>

to Ava

You are on thin ice with the gay community.

(JK JK LOL ROFL JK)

Specific instructions:

1) Wait for him to contact you.

2) Meet in a public place.

3) Ask him what he thinks this is. Make him answer this first. DO NOT LET HIM GET AWAY WITHOUT ANSWERING YOU. If he says, "the start of something" or "I want you to be my girlfriend," you can stay. If he says, "We're just having fun," leave. Not abruptly. But the first moment you can do so without it being a big deal.

a. If you are able to stay, make sure you have another talk about exclusivity before actual intercourse, but until that moment, just enjoy your first official relationship!

b. If you have to leave abruptly, do not hang out with him ever again one-on-one. Don't be rude or ignore him. Instead be "busy." He will either change his tune or sing a song you don't want anyway!

Please do not share this foolproof list with anyone. If you disobey, and credit its creation to me, I will deny everything.

**4:12 PM PST**

Jake just texted me!

To apologize for "passing out early."

Like a little bitch?

Yep! I said, "No problem."

These are like modern-day love letters.

I wonder if future college kids will study them in lit class.

What was I supposed to say back???

"NBD. Want to be my boyfriend??"

Couldn't hurt.

Should I ask to see him?

NO!!

He should ask to see you.

## IN COLD BLOOD

---

**Gen Goldman** <GENX1999@gmail.com>

to Ava

Have you seen this??? Article below!

**CASUAL BEACON PARTY MARRED BY FRESHMAN FUED**

By Genevieve Goldman

*Berkeley Beacon* Staff

BOSTON—A small congregation of *Beacon* employees gathered together Saturday night to celebrate a well-received issue only for the lively celebration to be interrupted by a screaming match between two cub reporters. Genevieve Goldman arrived at said party at approximately 9 PM. The group email cited 8 PM as the official start time. Kent Winzel, Goldman's editor, was hosting the party at his home in Allston, and directed his young guest and protégée to the beverages.

Upon entrance into the kitchen, Goldman immediately spotted fellow journalist and ne'er-do-well, Alex Cassidy. Cassidy was already a few drinks in and greeted his rumored rival with a smirk. Goldman, stone-cold sober, refused to take the bait and poured herself a modest glass of boxed wine before retiring to the living room.

After about an hour of stimulating conversation, Goldman went to refill her glass for the third (or fourth) time and found Cassidy still manning the table. Goldman inquired if Cassidy was hired help, and Cassidy shot back an accusation involving Goldman's roommate and questionable loyalty. Rumor has it that Goldman's roommate, Shannon Middleton, is gunning for a position on the Student Government Association (SGA). Seeing as the *Beacon* serves as the sole checks and balances for the SGA, there is often controversy surrounding any possible conflicts of interest.

Goldman, having no idea that her roommate was even running for SGA, lashed out and accused Cassidy of trying to start unnecessary trouble. Cassidy retaliated with faux concern that the *Beacon*'s reputation would be on the line if an unreliable editor were to be hired on staff. The argument continued at increasing volume until Winzel, Goldman's editor, entered the room and encouraged both parties to partake in the next round of Kings. Goldman obliged while Cassidy preferred to join a grating conversation about the semicolon. He could later be heard quoting Oscar Wilde from the other room.

The night proceeded without further incident until Goldman was on her way to the train and spotted

Cassidy a few feet ahead. Goldman didn't say anything until the two were waiting for the B Line train. She then asked Cassidy if he had had a good time, to which Cassidy scoffed and rolled his eyes. Goldman then inquired if she had done something to offend Cassidy, to which Cassidy reportedly replied, "You haven't done anything to me."

This unnerving statement hung in the air until the two young people boarded the train and found their way back to their dorms without further incident.

WHAT A PSYCHOPATH!!!

## Re: IN COLD BLOOD

---

**Ava Helmer** <AVA.HELMER@gmail.com>

to Gen

Not to edit you on your journalism, but from a storytelling point of view, I found this particular article anticlimactic. The headline was click bait and I was left unsatisfied. Who cares if Shannon is running for SGA? Why is "You've haven't done anything to me" an unnerving statement? What do you want to have done to him?

Honestly, it sounds like you want him to pull your hair on the playground so you can hit him back and then fall in love 15 years later.

## Re: IN COLD BLOOD

---

**Gen Goldman** <GENX1999@gmail.com>

to Ava

This isn't a rom-com. You don't understand the dynamic.

**9:12 PM EST**

I convinced Shannon not to run for SGA.

How?? Why??

I explained that she would have to go to a lot of long meetings.

She didn't already know that?

NOPE!

She's gonna join Quidditch instead.

I no longer believe this is a real school.

Eat shit, Alex.

**7:23 PM PST**

Jake wants me to come over to talk about the script . . .

Come over where?

I don't know. The secret library he keeps under his bed?

I'm assuming his room.

HEY! Don't take all your pent-up sexual frustration out on me.

I'm the wind beneath your wings.

Can I go?

I'm told this is a free country. For white men.

But you explicitly told me that I have to meet him in a public place.

Eh. Rules are meant to be broken.

YOU WROTE THOSE RULES.

Use a condom!

## SHANNON (A CHARACTER STUDY)

---

**Gen Goldman** <GENX1999@gmail.com>

to Ava

So I know you're probably busy making sweet, sweet third base right now, but I wanted to fill you in on what I'm doing with my night.

Since offering Shannon the sage advice of giving up her political career so I can advance mine, she seems to think we are friends. I spent the last hour listening to her dissect her relationship with Baseball Mike, even though it appears to have ended weeks ago, and also was never a relationship.

I began asking questions about her life, out of morbid curiosity instead of genuine concern, and learned that her family is even stranger than she is! Her dad "works for the government" but won't tell anyone how, and her mom is clearly in love with her female best friend. They go on "girl trips" half the year. Her younger brother is some sort of savant and has already graduated college, yet he works in a Starbucks???? Who are these people?! I think her entire family is lying to her about everything and she has no idea. At least I am well aware that my father is an alcoholic and my mother is a classic enabler. They still lie to me all the time, but I know better than to trust them!

Did I tell you my mom suddenly called me four times the other day? Like she randomly remembered she has an adult daughter? When I finally called back, she was reabsorbed in her second “miracle” child. Apparently Hope is flourishing in kindergarten and learned to express herself through finger paint? How can I listen to this sort of information with a straight face, knowing that my form of entertainment as a small kid was drawing on the wall with poop because no one was watching me?

ANYWAY . . .

Back to my case study: Shannon thinks Baseball Mike simply has intimacy issues and once he explores himself with (a bunch of) other girls, he will realize that they belong together. This journey of self-discovery includes hooking up with Shannon’s lifelong friend, Kelly, who goes to BU and met Mike THROUGH Shannon. Shannon isn’t mad, though, because she purposely stole Kelly’s boyfriend in 10th grade and karma is real. According to her savant brother. I’m a bit pissed I’ve wasted $7.99 on a Hulu subscription when I could have just been watching this strange creature in her natural habitat.

PEACE & MONKEYS,

Gen Goodall

P.S. I don't actually pay for Hulu. I use your account so please don't change the password.

P.P.S. When are we upgrading to no commercials?

## Re: SHANNON (A CHARACTER STUDY)

---

**Ava Helmer** <AVA.HELMER@gmail.com>

to Gen

My big takeaway from this is that your mom sucks. I hope I'm allowed to say that.

## Re: SHANNON (A CHARACTER STUDY)

---

**Gen Goldman** <GENX1999@gmail.com>

to Ava

Hahahaha, you are! But only because you're a survivor of that one awful trip to Disneyland.

RIP ICE CREAM MICKEY.

2:03 PM PST

You're not going to ask what happened??

I did ask what happened!

No. You gave a eulogy for an ice cream cone.

We have an open door policy. I don't have to ask. You can just tell.

No, because then I think you don't care, and I don't like to tell people things they don't care about.

That's one of the rules I learned in social skills class.

I CARE!

Not enough to ask.

Ava, will you please tell me every minute detail of your evening? Starting from sunset onward?

No. I'm busy.

You are more work than any of the girls I'm actually hooking up with!

Awwww. I love you too.

## MINUTIAE

---

**Ava Helmer** <AVA.HELMER@gmail.com>

to Gen

SO! I arrived at Jake's a few hours after sunset but I assume you were being sarcastic about that being your preferred starting time. (I did have a disgusting dinner, though. Remind me that I hate beets.)

When I got to Jake's room, his roommate, Tyler, was there smoking REEFER. He offered me some, but I declined since I wanted my wits about me. (And part of me is afraid that I will like weed so much I will become a big-time stoner and throw my life away.)

We all sat and chatted for a bit. Apparently Tyler is big on Instagram? Seems weird since he is VERY boring in person. He showed me a video of him skateboarding UP a ramp. It had one million views. I can only hope it's just his supportive mother watching it over and over again.

After a while, Jake told Tyler with his eyes to scram. I thought "talk about the script" meant "make out," but he actually had a lot of notes? He thinks his character comes off as gay because he doesn't want to have sex with Sophia. I tried to explain their lack of physical chemistry and the notion of a heightened reality, but he fought me pretty hard. He said I have a hard time writing male characters since I don't understand how much sex drives the male psyche.

That's when the night sort of took a turn because:

1) I was super offended that he thinks I don't know how to write believable male characters.

2) I became paranoid that all he thinks about is sex and the only reason he talks to me is sex, and I am not ready to have sex, so he will stop talking to me.

I had no choice but to ask him if he was speaking from personal experience:

JAKE: Of course.
AVA: Are you thinking about sex right now?
JAKE: Yeah. Are you?
AVA: Only because you brought it up! Have you . . . had it before?
JAKE (*laughs*): Yeah.

LONG BEAT

AVA: I have not.
JAKE: I figured.

And this is where I start to spiral. What about me screams virgin? Is it my hair? My clothes? My inability to talk about the act of sex without sounding like an alien attempting to mimic human behavior? OR! Even worse. What if it's my hand job giving? At this point I'm completely mortified when he says—

JAKE: You seem too busy.

WHAT?! I seem too busy?? I am painfully bored 1/3 of my life. And that includes the 1/3 I spend sleeping. What would give this person the impression that I am TOO BUSY to have intercourse? How long does it take???

AVA: What would give you that impression?
JAKE: I don't know. You seem like a serious person who is busy doing serious things. Even you in this house right now. Seems wrong.

HOW CAN HE PEER INTO MY SOUL AND SEE MY

DEEPEST FEARS??? Why am I unable to hide behind liquid eyeliner like everyone else???

AVA: I don't think I'm too serious. Was it not clear that this was a comedy script?
JAKE (*laughs again*): I don't mean you aren't funny. You just have a serious personality. Like an adult who is stuck going to college.
AVA: Is that bad?
JAKE: No! I like it. I'm also really mature for my age.

Then we started to kiss because I didn't know how to respond to that. TBH, I don't find him particularly mature . . . Anyway, our tongues started slapping and he tried to take my shirt off but I stopped him.

AVA: What does sex mean to you?
JAKE: In three words?
(*adorable slap that only slightly misses its mark*)
JAKE: I don't know. It depends on the person I am doing it with.
AVA: What would it mean if you did it with me?
JAKE: I think I would probably have to try it first to know.
(*another slap, not as adorable, much harder*)
AVA: I don't really want to do that if I don't know what this is.
(*lots of vague/crude hand gestures*)
JAKE: DTR?

That's not me abbreviating it. He said that out loud, nonironically, which honestly made the entire situation a lot less high-risk for me. I nodded, and then we had a confusing conversation that I wish I could relay word for word but unfortunately I was scrambling to keep up in the moment. I think the takeaway was that he is open to being in a relationship but doesn't think we are there yet? But if I don't want to have sex unless we are in a relationship, we can just hang out and not have sex.

How does this sound to an outside observer? To me it seems reasonable if not disappointing. He's not pressuring me and he's also right. We don't really know each other that well. There is no rush to be "boyfriend/girlfriend" and then regret it.

I *think* I agreed with him, and then he went down on me! It was . . . itchy?? Starting to think my body might be broken . . .

Send help and wisdom!

A

**Re: MINUTIAE**

---

**Gen Goldman** <GENX1999@gmail.com>

to Ava

Starting to think this guy is either super evolved or heavily manipulative. The comment about you not knowing how to write male characters pushes him over into manipulative town.

Please tell me that you are not going to change the script to accommodate his weak male ego. You are the writer. You have the vision. And everyone's sex drive is different. (Maybe his character is gay! Or a gray asexual! That's for you to decide.)

Here is a question: Why do you even want this guy to be your boyfriend? Is it just to have sex? Or do you really like him? Chinatownjake98?

## Re: MINUTIAE

**Ava Helmer** <AVA.HELMER@gmail.com>
to Gen

Those are some very good questions. And my answer is that I have no idea. How does anyone know why they are dating someone? I'm 18. I barely have a grasp on familial love. Most of my feelings and actions are completely hormonal (or chemical).

I do know that I want to have a boyfriend. I have always wanted that. Probably a bit too much, which is why none of them have wanted me. (If desperation was a cologne, I sprayed too much of it all of middle school.) The only thing that made me look incrementally cool in high school was being friends with you, something all of your other cool friends are still trying to figure out.

So now I suddenly have this guy *open* to the idea of dating me and I don't want to mess it up. Will I marry

Jake? No. Probably not. But I'm not just walking around accidentally bumping into love interests like you are. (Oops! There's another one! Whoops! Three-way collision.) I feel like I can't risk throwing this person away because he is not perfectly synced up to my time line.

I want to talk about it with my therapist, but I'm sure she will somehow turn the whole thing into my fault. Does that sound defensive? Because I'm definitely not defensive ;)

**5:13 PM EST**

HOLD UP!

What??

How did we not talk about the other thing?

What other thing?

👅👅👅

Gen! Gross!

I'm in class. I can't talk about this.

You're always "in class."

OPEN YOUR MIND.

TOUCH YOURSELF.

Airplane mode.

## MENAGE & NOSH

---

**Gen Goldman** <GENX1999@gmail.com>

to Ava

At approximately 7:55 PM, I was returning to my dorm to continue my study of Strange Shannon in the wild, when Charlotte called me. Yes, she called because she is an adult and I am a child who hit Ignore by accident. I texted her back because, despite all my talk, I am weak and afraid. She wrote back and invited me over to her apartment to watch a movie.

In case you suffered severe memory loss, this is the universal signal for "hook up" (i.e., Netflix and Chill). So I hopped on the train, gulped down a couple Orbit mints, and headed over, thinking I would find her scantily clad in a nonappropriated kimono.

Instead, I found her completely clothed and standing next to her nerdy friend, Tom. Tom is a TA in Dramaturgy because he tried to be a theater actor and failed. Tom is also super cute. I immediately liked Tom.

Charlotte invites me in, sneezing in the process. She's sick and wants company so if she dies, someone will call her parents and yell at them for not being more supportive. I'm a bit confused about my presence, until I realize she must have called everyone in the first few scrolls of her contacts. I try not to take it personally and instead enjoy a delicious slice of pecan pie that Tom BAKED. Have I mentioned that I like Tom?

About an hour goes by of us talking and not deciding what to watch when Charlotte announces she needs to take a nap. It's around 9:30. Seems like that's just going to bed early, but who am I to say? She tells me and Tom not to leave, because she has snacks and doesn't want to wake up to an empty house. (She is still under the impression that she is taking a nap.)

We shrug and turn on a movie, perfectly comfortable with this idea. Charlotte has a way of normalizing any and all behavior. As soon as she leaves the room, Tom asks if I want a blanket. You know me. My body radiates heat, but it seemed rude to say no. Also I wanted to see what it would feel like for a grown man I am not related to to put a blanket on me. The answer: sexy.

Suddenly, I find myself cuddling with a male stranger in my female lover's living room. I ask Tom how long he's known Charlotte, and he replies, "A long time." I ask him how well he knows her, and he replies, "Not as well as you." I must have blushed because he assured me that I wasn't giving it away. I'm just so clearly Charlotte's type. He knows because they have the same type.

YEP! THAT'S WHAT HE SAID! TALK ABOUT A LINE! THAT WORKED!

We made out for about forever. All clothes were kept on in an attempt at decency. We could hear Charlotte snoring from the next room . . .

Sometime around 2 AM, Tom untangled himself from me and the blanket and announced that he was escorting me home. I assumed that meant he was inviting himself over into my twin bed, but he really meant that he was just escorting me home. As soon as I tried to explain to him the best way to sneak into my room without awakening the beast, he laughed and kissed me goodbye. He then announced he would get my info from Charlotte, which seems weird but convenient.

Anyway. That was my night. He looks like a male Ellen Page to give you some visuals.

Also, I am currently obsessed with this song: "Just 2 Guyz."

I'm Guy #1

## Re: MENAGE & NOSH

---

**Ava Helmer** <AVA.HELMER@gmail.com>

to Gen

OK. I am confused. You like guys again?? Or is this an anomaly? Maybe you just like forbidden authority types. That would make sense considering your gross flirtation with Security Officer Peters.

Do you still like Charlotte? She seems a bit crazy. Who throws a party so she doesn't have to be alone when she's sick??

I'm confused. But I guess I'm always confused.

Please don't yell at me.

A

**Re: MENAGE & NOSH**

---

**Gen Goldman** <GENX1999@gmail.com>

to Ava

Hahaha. I never stopped liking guys. I'm just 90–10 at this point. And he has a very feminine energy.

**Re: MENAGE & NOSH**

---

**Ava Helmer** <AVA.HELMER@gmail.com>

to Gen

OK. Cool.

I WANT TO BE GUY #1!

**7:57 PM EST**

I can see Kent's belly button.

Who is Kent?

Oh, sry. Kent, my editor.

Why can you see his belly button? Is he not wearing a shirt?

There is a shirt. It is too small.

On purpose?

Unclear.

Keep me updated.

I think I spotted a small piece of lint.

Unsubscribe from all updates.

## THE EGO AND THE ID

---

**Ava Helmer** <AVA.HELMER@gmail.com>

to Gen

I think Dr. Lily might be clinically insane. How can I tell my therapist she needs a therapist? She probably already has one who is equally useless.

After my session, I looked up sadistic tendencies. They include deriving pleasure from inflicting pain, suffering, or humiliation on others. This seems about right!

I can't tell if Dr. Lily is intentionally trying to drive me crazy, or if she has no idea what she is doing and therefore relies solely on condescending looks and low murmurs of disapproval.

I went in ready to discuss my relationship with Jake, and she immediately started asking me questions about my family. My family is not the problem. My family is the only reason I am still alive.

Instead of spending the forty minutes creating a strategy to move forward, Dr. Lily wanted to know if my father put unnecessary pressure on me to succeed.

SERIOUSLY? Is this your first day?

I kept trying to steer the conversation back to my actual dilemma (what I should do about this person who wants to hook up but not commit), but she kept attaching merit to the fact that my dad gave away our dog. I only mentioned this as the ONE TIME my father disappointed me, and she latched on to it with an iron fist. Honestly, it seems like she probably has daddy issues.

With ten minutes left, I (loudly) announced that I need to talk about Jake because I can't go another week without coping strategies for this uncertainty. Gray areas make me nauseous. Anyone who listens to me for more than five minutes knows that.

Instead of listening to my needs, she insisted that I was avoiding talking about my family. What is there to avoid? The fact that for 18 years my parents have been my best friends (current company aside), and all of my problems come from other external circumstances as well as a chemical imbalance in my brain?

I have been in therapy four times longer than you've even been a therapist, Lily! When your patient is begging for help, help her!

So what did she do?

Asked me another question about the dumb dog. (May

she rest in peace with that terrible family in Riverside.) So I left. Yep. With eight minutes left, I stormed out and gently screamed that I would not be returning. I can't go back to her. She is making it all worse. I need to call my mom and figure something else out. I need to see an actual doctor and not someone who is barely old enough to drink.

I hate this person, Gen. I literally hate her and can feel the rage surging through my body. I hope she gets fired and has her mouth sewn shut. I'm not even back at my dorm yet while I'm typing this and it's so obvious that I've been crying. Thank god for university anonymity. Could not have survived a small school.

Oh, fuck, here comes one of my "sisters." I hate my life.

## Re: THE EGO AND THE ID

**Gen Goldman** <GENX1999@gmail.com>

to Ava

Are you OK? I just tried to call you a couple times but you didn't answer. Maybe you're talking to your mom.

I'm so sorry, babe. I wish I was there so I could beat the doctor's ass and take away all her (loose) credentials. Can you ask for another doctor on campus? Or is it better to just see someone off campus? Either way, I think you should get all of your money back AND they should pay you for emotional damages.

Have you thought about going back on meds to help with the anxiety? I know you hate them, but maybe a low dose of a different kind? Or maybe, bear with me, weed? Seriously. Go get a card and try a little indica? It's not even illegal anymore!

And when it comes to Jake, if the gray area is driving you crazy, you don't have to stay there. Tell him to shit or get off the pot. It's first semester, freshman year. There are plenty of other mediocre men out there to torment you.

LOVE YOU! GET SOME ICE CREAM!

G

**6:43 PM PST**

Hey. Sorry I missed your calls. Was talking to my mom.

It's OK! What she say?

That I can find someone else. It's too late to get a car for this semester. All the parking passes are taken, but my mom said she would drive me.

That's nice. Are you going to go back to your old one?

No. Tina, the girl I ran into when I was crying, suggested someone closer.

GASP! A sorority girl doesn't have a perfect life!

Alert the media!

Stop. She was nice.

And I'm not in one of the cool sororities where everyone has a perfect life.

Those houses dropped me, remember?

Ah, yes. PIE IN UR FACE HOUSE. How could I forget. They r on my hit list.

Right after Dr. Lily.

I appreciate it.

I feel a bit dumb that my mom is going to come pick me up from college once a week.

Don't feel dumb! That's a #diva lifestyle. OWN IT.

OY.

## WOODWARD & BERNSTEIN

---

**Gen Goldman** <GENX1999@gmail.com>

to Ava

In the continuing saga that is the *Berkeley Beacon,* Alex and I just got paired up for an investigative article about Emerson's tightening security. Rumor has it the president is taking meetings with various security companies to come up with a plan intended to limit shootings and stuff.

Pretty soon we'll all be asked to walk naked through a metal detector in order to get to class. I plan to peacefully abstain. And then maybe drop out.

I have no idea why we're being teamed up for this. My only guess is an insatiable need for office drama? Kent, my editor, insists we need to work together to remain objective since I am anti-police state and Alex is an idiot.

That might be a little harsh. He's a Boston native and I guess the bombing really shook up his whole family. He thinks it's fine to give up all rights and privacy if it will save ONE life. I couldn't disagree more. What's the point of living if you don't have any rights or privacy?? How can he not see that, especially when he's trans? Has he never interacted with the TSA?

The worst part of the whole thing was that he acted excited to work with me. Like it isn't obvious to everyone that he hates my guts. So then I seemed like an asshole when I immediately fought Kent, my editor, and tried to get the assignment myself. Everyone looked at me like I was petty, but I really think two reporters will just slow down the story and students have a right to know about all this before they wake up to drug dogs in their underwear drawer.

Kent, my editor, shot down my attempt at flying solo and encouraged us to think of each other as colleagues and not competitors. BARF. After the meeting, Alex wanted to hang out to strategize, but I told him I had an early class. We're meeting up later today. I need time to figure out how to play this. Maybe I'll give him back what's he's giving me: condescending aloofness.

I just hope my name comes first in the byline.

KIDDING. It's alphabetical. I'm fucked.

## Re: WOODWARD & BERNSTEIN

**Ava Helmer** <AVA.HELMER@gmail.com>

to Gen

Yikes. Not the best situation. My only advice is kill 'em with kindness. Maybe this is a test and Kent wants to see how you work with unreasonable people? Make him the difficult one. Just do your job the best that you can and compliment his shoes or something. I always compliment people I can't stand. It throws them off and makes me feel like a better person despite the hate and judgment in my heart.

You can get through this. You will get through this.

What is his Instagram handle so I can hate follow?

## Re: WOODWARD & BERNSTEIN

**Gen Goldman** <GENX1999@gmail.com>

to Ava

@CassidyKid. But it's private because he is the worst.

**9:21 PM PST**

I did a bad thing.

How bad? White girl cornrow bad?
Or Scientology bad?

Too bad to make a joke!
I ruined all the stuff.
Are you in jail?
No!
Then it's not that bad.
Can you talk?
Not really. I'm at this dumb party and I can't hear anything.
OK.
Will call in morning.
♥♥♥♥♥♥

## SIGNING OFF

**Ava Helmer** <AVA.HELMER@gmail.com>
to Gen

I know you are out having the time of your life, but I need to ask you a serious question. Have I always been the dumbest person you know? Or did I hide my stupidity with misleading data like a high SAT score and expensive clothes? I feel like the world's biggest moron and, as such, I am also the last to know (that I am the world's biggest moron).

Last night I started freaking out about the whole Jake thing. We are shooting the short next weekend, and I felt like I needed to have a better handle on our relationship before working together in front of a group that includes my parents. We already had plans to hang out tomorrow night, but I couldn't wait that long for clarity so I texted him. Seven times. Turns out, not a lucky number when you are a girl with zero fucking chill. He finally responded that he was just getting out of a late class. I told him to come over because Jessica was out, which MIGHT have given the wrong impression. He arrived five minutes later and I was crying.

Yep. I was crying. So Jake, being a normal, chill person, assumed something was really wrong. Like a death in the family. Or a plagiarism accusation (apparently USC is really cracking down on ripping off B movies no one has seen). I had to explain that nothing was wrong. Other than the fact that he doesn't want to be my boyfriend.

If you are too embarrassed on my behalf, you can stop reading because it only gets worse.

After a FULL MINUTE of silence, he said, "I thought we already talked about this."

Cue the waterworks! In case it wasn't already clear to everyone in my hall that I was sobbing. The increased flow of my tears only freaked him out more as he scrambled to explain a fear of commitment and literally said, "It's not you, it's me."

I kept mumbling that I really liked him and think we could be happy together, while he searched around for an escape route. Once I calmed down enough to breathe, I explained that I have issues with anxiety. He started to be more understanding and less freaked out. But he still didn't want to be my boyfriend. (Can't imagine why! Who doesn't want a clingy, desperate A-cup following them around?)

He left like ten minutes later, having decided we should stop hooking up since it would complicate the movie. I was shocked he still wanted to be in the movie. That seems weird right??

WHAT IS WRONG WITH ME?? And why can I not stop crying?

## Re: SIGNING OFF

---

**Gen Goldman** <GENX1999@gmail.com>

to Ava

Ava!!!! No!!! Please don't cry! I'm sorry I couldn't talk last night! You need to text me code tears when there are tears!

Honestly, I don't think that what happened is SO bad. Like is it cringeworthy? Yes. But will it have long-term repercussions on your life? Absolutely not.

If anything, this whole exchange just made Jake look bad. What kind of man can't handle a few tears? A boy, that's who! (Sorry. I couldn't think of a better metaphor or saying.) Seriously, this is very revealing about his character. It's better to know this now. Don't take this the wrong way, but you aren't going to be a "low-maintenance" girlfriend. But there is no reason you should be! You are an emotional person and you need to be with someone who has the faculties to handle that. Jake does not sound like that guy . . .

In terms of practical next steps, you don't owe this guy anything. Other than your oral virginity. If you don't want him in your movie, cast someone else! You are the auteur! He is a piece of shit!

## Re: SIGNING OFF

---

**Ava Helmer** <AVA.HELMER@gmail.com>

to Gen

I love how you somehow manage to take my side regardless of how despicable my behavior. I'm too afraid to recast him. I would rather attempt to play it cool and act as though he isn't the only guy who has seen me naked.

## TREATY OF VERSAILLES

---

**Gen Goldman** <GENX1999@gmail.com>

to Ava

Operation Make Alex Look Bad is in full swing. I have now met up with him twice, and both times I was the pinnacle of politeness. Turns out, I do have manners. I guess my rudeness has been a choice and not the product of a poor upbringing. I even bit my tongue when he suggested it was a GOOD IDEA the NSA can read our emails.

He insisted that we meet at his place, which is an off-campus apartment in Beacon Hill (for snobs). The whole place was decorated as though the person who lives there has a good personality, so I have to credit it to his roommate, who was MIA and probably more interesting. We spent the first hour or so talking about everyone at the paper, which was fun, and then we started arguing about the assignment in a very passive-aggressive, adult way. Our second meetup was even more heated, but I kept my cool and made him feel dumb at least once. Instead of attacking, I pulled a Dr. Lily and asked "Why?" 4,000 times until his logic started to crack.

We're splitting up the research, but he still wants to make calls in the same room. He's obviously very suspicious and wants to hear (and steal) all of my questions.

I found out Alex also has Charlotte as a TA but thinks she is a "flake posturing as a serious journalist." I resisted informing him that that flake has a great ass!

You would be proud of me. I'm keeping all my feels on the inside, like a WASP.

*"Those who would give up liberty for security deserve neither."*—Genevieve Franklin

P.S. What happened to our quote thing??? I miss us.

## Re: TREATY OF VERSAILLES

---

**Ava Helmer** <AVA.HELMER@gmail.com>

to Gen

I'm very proud of you. You are posturing as a normal person not consumed by rage.

Here is a crazy idea. Have you ever thought that Alex wants to work in the same room as you because he likes you? Like likes you? Or is he gay? (Is that the proper terminology for a trans man? Please don't yell at me.)

*"Confidence is 10% hard work and 90% delusion."*
—Ava Fey

## Re: TREATY OF VERSAILLES

---

**Gen Goldman** <GENX1999@gmail.com>

to Ava

Hahahahaha. That is the right terminology but the wrong interpretation. There is nothing romantic going on here. I'm barely attracted to him, and I'm attracted to everyone. I find his personality off-putting (even if his face is inviting). We are at war. And only one of us will survive!

*"It takes a lot of money to look this cheap."*—G. G. Parton

**4:13 PM PST**

Emma is dropping out!

Which one is Emma again?

My cool theater major British friend!

Oh! That Emma.

She's dropping out of college?

No! Of the house!

Y?

She thinks it's all "rubbish." Because she is British.

I'm so pissed. She was my only real friend here.

Are you going to drop out too?

No.

I don't know. Should I?

Maybe try talking to a few other people first.

WHY DOES EVERYTHING BAD ALWAYS HAPPEN TO ME?!

This isn't Brexit, Ava. Chill out.

SORRY! I know that phrase is a trigger for you.

Chill out. (Not Brexit.)

**8:42 PM EST**

Tom wants to take me on a proper date???

Men are so dumb.

I thought you liked Tom.

I do. So why waste money on me?

Ask to go somewhere fancy!

DUH!

## HEARTS OF DARKNESS: A FILMMAKER'S APOCALYPSE

**Ava Helmer** <AVA.HELMER@gmail.com>

to Gen

It's finally arrived. D-day. Call time is 8 AM. We start in my dorm room and then move outside. Sunday we spend the entire day at my house. Both my parents have offered to be PAs, although my dad asked for an executive producer credit because he is paying my tuition. I think I'll give it to him so he has something to hang on to in his old age.

I haven't see or spoken to Jake outside of call sheet emails. I have no idea how to act or behave tomorrow. I guess like a director who has better things to worry about than her romantic future? I'm just glad this whole short is based on a LACK of chemistry between the two leads. If I had to see Jake and Sophia actually hitting it off for two full days, I think I would blow my brains out.

Going to try to get some sleep. Yes. I know it's only 9 PM. Make fun of me later.

**Re: HEARTS OF DARKNESS: A FILMMAKER'S APOCALYPSE**

---

**Gen Goldman** <GENX1999@gmail.com>

to Ava

KATHRYN BIGELOW WINS BEST DIRECTING: 2010 OSCARS

Go get 'em, kid!

**2:04 PM EST**

How's it going???

**5:37 PM EST**

I hope ur crushing it and not suddenly mad at me for something I did 3 years ago.

**8:29 PM EST**

Sending you positive vibes!!

**9:37 PM PST**

Thank you!! Day 1 down!

How did it go??

2 tired 2 type.

Whoa.

**11:42 AM EST**

Ur mom just sent me a hot pic of you directing.

👌

**6:51 PM PST**

Did I look dumb??

No! Adorable!

I mean . . . badass and professional.

This has been the craziest weekend.

Still not done.

I want a full report.

If I survive . . .

What are you doing?

Fancy date with cis male.

OOOOOOOOOOO

**LADY & THE TRAMP (I'M THE TRAMP)**

---

**Gen Goldman** <GENX1999@gmail.com>

to Ava

Tom is a hilarious attempt at a person. He is 26 but acts 45. He brought me a dandelion as a gift. Also, he rides a Vespa. So I can cross riding a Vespa off my nonexistent bucket list. He tried to make me wear a helmet, but I ain't about that life.

After a few near-death intersections, we arrived at some pricey Italian joint where all the waiters pretended to be Italian. Tom talked to them in a French accent just to keep the feel "international." We ordered pastas and wine, and when they asked to see my ID, Tom laughed and said, "That's got to feel good!" This caused us all to laugh and the waiter to forget the basic rules of running a drinking establishment.

Dinner was fun. I ate all of mine and half of Tom's. Got to love free stuff and a date with a small appetite!

We left the restaurant and started walking around. Tom had heard about some art installation, but I didn't want him to think we were dating so I asked to have sex instead. I am basically a manic pixie nightmare. He swallowed hard and then tried to hand me a helmet AGAIN. Boys never learn. We got to his place and I took off my own clothes because he seems like someone with shaky hands and I hate pretending not to notice people fucking up. He then took off his cardigan, which felt like a big move. He asked if I wanted coffee. WHILE I WAS NAKED. I said sure. We had naked coffee and then kissed. And then we ate miniature scones one of his lovesick students baked for him.

After an unreasonably long amount of time sitting bare-assed on a wicker chair, we finally got busy. It was OK. The scones were better. I didn't sleep over because I thought it would be funnier to leave.

Charlotte texted me this morning. She's pretending not to know what's up, but we all know what's up and IT'S ME.

*"Be so good they can't ignore you."*—G. Martin

## Re: LADY & THE TRAMP (I'M THE TRAMP)

---

**Ava Helmer** <AVA.HELMER@gmail.com>

to Gen

Are you just trying to fill some sort of weird sex quota? Why are you having sex with people you don't even like? Not that you shouldn't like Tom, he actually sounds adorable. I feel sad for Tom. And me. I should be with Tom. Give him my number and stop having emotionally unavailable intercourse with him.

**3:44 PM EST**

If you get a text from a 603 #, it's Tom.

WHAT? Why?

You told me to give him your number.
I was joking. And delirious.
Oh, right! Still waiting on my full write-up.
Need a nap then will send.
Dope.
Tom digs your Insta.
You are a monster!

**PARADISE LOST**

---

**Ava Helmer** <AVA.HELMER@gmail.com>
to Gen

So many things happened in the last 24 hours, I'm not sure where to start or end. I guess the biggest takeaway is that we finished! We got all the shots and all the scenes and all the lines. There was some dialogue that Sophia kept bumping on, so I played it super cool and told her to rewrite it "in her character's voice." (Don't worry, I will retain sole writing credit.) Curtis and I worked great together. He brought his girlfriend, Darcy, as a PA and she was super helpful, although she spent most of yesterday talking to my parents. Ruth and Ken had a blast, by the way. My mom decided she would be in charge of crafty and made a series of inedible dips. My dad kept asking Curtis where to move the lights and offered a plethora of extension cords. It was maximum-level adorable. The shoot ended with a Helmer-sponsored pizza party. What a night to remember!

Professionally, I think I handled myself well. There were a

few minor freak-outs (like when Emma spilled soda on her one outfit), but I tried to keep the anxiety on the inside! Curtis helped a lot because he is one of those people you could actually describe as "centered." I hope to work exclusively with him for the remainder of my career. (He doesn't know this yet. I am trying not to come on too strong.)

Personally, I was a COMPLETE MESS. Before the shoot, I decided to not engage. I would be civil but not friendly. Nice but aloof. In control, not spiraling. I assumed Jake would be the same. NOPE. Jake was a complete flirt. And not just to me. He spent the entire weekend leapfrogging between Sophia and me. I think he had his hand on someone's back at all times. It was infuriating! At first I thought he was doing this to punish me in some way? But then I realized it wasn't intentional. He just loves attention. And Sophia gave it to him. Even my mom laughed at all his dumb jokes! I wanted to vomit!

I can't believe I ever liked him. I can't believe I STILL like him. If only Curtis didn't have a girlfriend and was physically attractive.

Maybe I will just be a recluse filmmaker who never marries but has her finger on the pulse of human emotion despite never experiencing anything other than third base.

*"Life is suffering."*—Budd-va

P.S. Tom didn't even text me. My life is pathetic.

**Re: PARADISE LOST**

**Gen Goldman** <GENX1999@gmail.com>

to Ava

Not to minimize the bastardness that is chinatownjake98, but my big takeaway from this is your parents throwing a wrap pizza party. I can just see them at the Oscars in a few years, handing out gift bags with your face on it. At what point will they quit their jobs and start working for you full time?

I am so proud of you, sweet baby angel! I can't wait to see a cut! What are you going to do with it? You should post it on YouTube! YouTube can change lives! You could go viral!

Try to forget about Jake. You officially don't have to see or worry about him anymore. (Except in the editing room, but I'm sure he will look bad on screen due to his small head.)

*"You made a movie!!"*—Genevieve Goldman to Ava Helmer, 2017

P.S. I didn't actually give Tom your phone number. I'm not a psycho.

P.P.S. Although I can if you want.

12:08 AM EST

Just had a thought.

Congratulations!

Funny.

Did your parents really not know about you and Jake the whole time?

Ha! Yeah, right!

They knew everything! That's why I was especially mad at my mom for having no loyalty.

Everything???

Gross, no.

PG version.

Do you think you will ever keep anything from them ever?

I kept the fingering to myself!

Proud of you.

## THE MAN

**Gen Goldman** <GENX1999@gmail.com>

to Ava

And by the man, I mean my editor, Kent. I went into the office to run my ideas for the security article past him, and he asked where Alex was. I shrugged. I am not his keeper. Kent then let out that disappointed-dad sigh, which I only recognized from the movies because my dad is too out of it to be disappointed. Kent then launched into a tirade about teamwork and subconscious sabotage?? He seems to think I am intentionally making enemies at the *Beacon* so I have someone to blame if I don't make staff. (Don't freak, I am still going to make staff.) He told me I should let my work speak for itself and not get bogged down in office politics. So I immediately asked, "What has Alex been saying?" And then he LAUGHED IN MY FACE. He thought this question proved my paranoia since Alex has said NOTHING about me. What a fucking power move.

I immediately switched gears and pledged my undying loyalty to the paper, the student body, and my country. He told me to stop being a smart-ass.

The meeting ended with him telling me to come back, WITH Alex, if I wanted to talk about the article.

Did I mention that I could see his chest hair the whole time? He really needs to get better-fitting clothes.

**Re: THE MAN**

---

**Ava Helmer** <AVA.HELMER@gmail.com>

to Gen

I don't know how to respond to this without setting you off, so just imagine I am sitting next to you, nodding my support and gently touching your arm.

11:36 PM EST

What was that about?

Nothing . . .

When have I ever been set off?

Um . . .

Whenever a male or authority figure tells you what to do.

So you think Kent had a right to yell at me?

Did he yell? Or did he talk?

Like a patronizing little bitch voice is any better than a yell.

I don't care about Kent. I'm just saying sometimes you overreact. I can't say whether or not that happened here because I wasn't there.

Right. You weren't.

How long you gonna be mad about this?

TBD.

I'll wait. ♥

## REMEMBER ME

---

**Ava Helmer** <AVA.HELMER@gmail.com>

to Gen

Hey, It's Ava. Helmer. From all those years of being your best friend. I just wanted to reach out and say, hey! I think you are really great and here is a list of why I am really great too!

1) Super accessible for all of your friendship needs. Sparse social calendar and lots of free time mean I'm able to put you first.

2) Brutal honesty. Almost (definitely) compulsively honest. So honest you will never have to ask for my opinion because I offer it without thinking.

3) Cool parents who love to buy you T-shirts with funny sayings. Free pizza parties also included.

4) Terrible style. In no danger of me asking to borrow your clothes because I can't pull them off. Nor would I want to.

5) Super needy, which makes you feel needed. Not ready for kids but want the responsibility of emotionally caring for a human being? Ava is the friend for you!

Hope you enjoyed your BFF refresher! I'll be here, three hours behind, eagerly awaiting your response.

*"What is a friend? A single soul dwelling in two bodies."*—Ava-totle

**Re: REMEMBER ME?**

---

**Gen Goldman** <GENX1999@gmail.com>

to Ava

It's been 3 HOURS! You're obsessed with me.

LOVE AND BLOOD,

G

4:31 PM EST

Alex called me and wants to "talk."

Do you think my editor ratted me out?

What do I get if I guess correctly?

What? Nothing.

Not worth the risk of being wrong.

I'm in it to win it.

You are not helping.

Just call him back.

I'll text him.

## MY FATHER, THE FAILURE

**Gen Goldman** <GENX1999@gmail.com>

to Ava

I don't know what's in the water (other than too much fluoride), but I just got another unexpected phone call. This time it was my father. He really needed to talk to me because he had record-breaking news: he is finally going to get sober!

I found this interesting because long-time fans and followers of the Goldman family might recall him saying something similar in 1999, 2004, summer of 2007, court-mandated winter of 2007, 2010, 2014, and last month. Although the most recent one was delivered in a boisterous, drunken fashion as some sort of sick joke?

You can imagine my skepticism at receiving this news, which set him off. How can I not believe in him? How will he have the strength to battle his disease without the support of those dearest to his heart?

Friends and followers, you might pause at this sort of “fruity” language. I certainly did. My father is more likely to shout out slightly racist slurs than messages of love. When I pointed this out, he sighed a breath full of wisdom and patience he doesn’t deserve. Apparently he is now a friend of Bill W. and living his life for a higher power. (Bill W. is a code word for AA, FYI. In case you didn’t grow up in a broken home.)

I asked him how long he’s been on this journey, and he replied, “Tomorrow is my anniversary. My one-week anniversary.”

ARE YOU KIDDING ME? CHECK IN AGAIN IN 1 YEAR. OR 3.

He’s trying to do 90 meetings in 90 days and he has this full-time sponsor, Breeze (given name Ralph). Breeze doesn’t think the meetings are enough, though, and is encouraging my father to meditate 2 hours a day, which should fit nicely into his schedule of doing nothing.

My mother hasn’t met Breeze yet, but she thinks he sounds like a wonderful influence. She is SO happy my father finally listened to her about AA. It’s not really a victory when it takes 20+years, but literally no one is asking for my opinion.

I was pretty dismissive on the call (I guess they expected exuberance), and somehow I ended up getting a lecture about life from a guy who hasn't been sober for any of it. Did you know that I need to open up my heart to the light and goodness of other people? Did you also know that my father once crashed his car into the giant menorah in front of our synagogue?

I'm really glad my dad is getting sober in time not to completely ruin Hope's childhood. He said having a daughter finally made him realize he needs to be a better man. I AM YOUR DAUGHTER. I HAVE BEEN YOUR DAUGHTER FOR 18 YEARS.

They're making me FaceTime Hope later so she doesn't have the mental repercussions of being an only child??? Apparently that is a thing my mother has been actively reading about. My existence in their life is purely service based.

I finally hung up the phone after what seemed like an eternity but was actually only 7 minutes. That seems like the best way to sum up my entire life with them.

Looking forward to NOT accepting his 9th-step apology.

BTW. Alex just wanted to invite me to a party. What a PSYCHO.

## Re: MY FATHER, THE FAILURE

**Ava Helmer** <AVA.HELMER@gmail.com>
to Gen

Wow. Mark Goldman, everyone. Even when you're across the country, he somehow has to make your life about him. It would be commendable if it wasn't so evil.

I don't know how you handle them in a civilized fashion. I would have run away at 10. I did run away at 10 and my parents are wonderful.

I'm so sorry about all this bullshit. I guess we can only hope he falls off the wagon quickly so he'll stop calling? Is that too dark? May the force be with him.

At least Hope is cute. Not as cute as you, but PRETTY cute. Maybe once you graduate, you can pretend she was a teen pregnancy and claim her as your own.

Are you going to Alex's party? Might be an olive branch. Or an elaborate setup for your humiliation. I only said the last part so you couldn't say it first.

**10:36 PM EST**

Currently at Alex's party.

Charlotte is here.

WHAT?!

I thought Alex hated Charlotte?

???

Maybe she's friends with his roommate?
How big is the party??
Small. 10 people.
Alex is being weird.
How?
Friendly. He must be drunk.
Be nice!
WHY
What are you doing?
Going to Jake's.
WHAT
WHY
Unclear.
Don't go!
It's too late. We just made eye contact!
I'm going in!
NOOOOOOOOOOOOOOOOOOOOOOOO

**12:13 AM EST**

What happened??
Did he kill you??
JAKE, IF YOU ARE READING THIS, I AM COMING FOR YOU.
I HAVE A PARTICULAR SET OF SKILLS.

**11:57 AM PST**

Alive and happy!
All good things.
NOW I AM VERY SUSPICIOUS!

## M. NIGHT SHYAMALAN TWIST

---

**Ava Helmer** <AVA.HELMER@gmail.com>

to Gen

In an epic turn of events, Jake is now my boyfriend. How is that for a headline?

Yep. I have a boyfriend. An actual boyfriend and not an elaborate setup organized by a frenemy at summer camp.

How did this happen? I have no idea. If you told me you had wired Jake money to commit to me, I would believe you.

Things were confusing on the shoot, as previously mentioned. Since then he's sent like one "check in about the footage" text, and I barely responded. Then last night he CALLED me and asked me to come over to "talk."

I assumed this was a thinly veiled booty call but was lonely so agreed. When I got there, he sat me down, very serious, and took my hands. He thanked me for giving him space and being patient. The time and perspective let him realize that what we have is special and he wants to give this (us) a real shot.

WHAT! ARE YOU KIDDING ME?? I searched the room for cameras, wondering if this was a prank video since his roommate is a big deal on social media. I couldn't find any, so I had to assume he was being sincere.

The last time a boy told me he liked me to my face I was 15 and the boy was 12. (Brad Karp. My weird neighbor who has recently become mega-cute.) I said "ew" and ran away.

If we are being completely honest, I sort of wanted to respond the same way. I've been obsessed with Jake since we met, but the moment he opened up and seemed sincere, something inside of me clenched. And not in a good way. Why would someone want to date me? He must be a big-time loser.

I KNOW. I'm the best. Everyone is perfect. Love is love.

Flip side. I'm a mentally unstable flatty who can't wear real pants because they hurt my stomach. What would a genuinely cool guy want with me?

Luckily, Jake didn't even wait for a response and instead started kissing me. I guess he assumed I was in shock from happiness? I'm glad that shock is hard to decipher.

Things escalated quickly from there. I think within three minutes he was reaching for a condom. I told him to stop.

SPOILER: I'm pregnant.

JUST KIDDING! I told him I wanted our first time to be special, and I wasn't clean enough. Yep. That was both an excuse and a real fear. I don't like anyone to touch my legs if I haven't shaved in the last two hours. OCD or Jewish genes? Your guess is as good as mine.

He said he understood. His room isn't the most romantic

spot on Greek Row. (I wonder what is.) He then asked for a blow job . . .

I'll save you the disgusting heteronormative details, but I think I did OK. I didn't get lockjaw or throw up, so that was a victory. He asked me to sleep over, but I was in the middle of a mild anxiety attack and said I couldn't. He kissed me good-bye and fell asleep before I left. (It was only 9:30. Maybe we have more in common than I thought.)

So. I have a boyfriend? Let me know if I seem different.

**Re: M. NIGHT SHYAMALAN TWIST**

---

**Gen Goldman** <GENX1999@gmail.com>

to Ava

HOLY SHIT! You had a dick in your mouth! That is so gross. I am never talking to you again.

**Re: M. NIGHT SHYAMALAN TWIST**

---

**Ava Helmer** <AVA.HELMER@gmail.com>

to Gen

Hahahahahahahaahh

**8:31 PM EST**

Are people treating you differently now that you're in a boring monogamous relationship?

Yes. I no longer have to pay for anything because people pity me too much.

4 real, though. You happy?

I think so!

Nervous about 👉👌.

U don't have to do it if ur nervous.

Yes I do! He's my boyfriend.

Who cares?

Probably him.

Eh. Let him not get what he wants for once in his privileged white life.

He's a quarter Spanish.

## BRITNEY SPEARS 2007

---

**Gen Goldman** <GENX1999@gmail.com>

to Ava

Just met up with Alex to finalize the article and it was like walking into a blizzard. That dude was COLD.

I don't know what changed between last night and today, but he completely shut me out. I tried to be friendly and speak out loud. In full sentences. Like an adult. Alex could not be bothered to return the favor.

I spent the uncomfortable 40 minutes replaying the party in my head, and the only thing I could think of is maybe he is into Charlotte. (I went home with Charlotte.) But that doesn't make sense because he hates Charlotte. Or maybe he only said he hated Charlotte because he doesn't want me to know he likes her? I don't think Charlotte would be into a trans man anyway. She's said some pretty questionable things about all-women festivals and including T in LGBT. I don't know. It would be weird if Alex was into a slightly transphobic person. But maybe I'm interpreting the situation all wrong.

Either way. I'm glad this "group project" is over. Writing is a lonely life and I prefer it that way.

How's your *boy*friend?

## Re: BRITNEY SPEARS 2007

---

**Ava Helmer** <AVA.HELMER@gmail.com>

to Gen

I think it's safe to say you are interpreting this entire situation wrong. Here is what it looks like from an outsider perspective.

Gen starts working at the paper. Gen meets cute boy who negs her. After a bit of negging, cute boy moves on to more outward forms of flirtation. Cute boy invites Gen to party at his house. Gen leaves with another woman, who cute boy already hates. Cute boy is sad and mad. Gen remains oblivious.

And Charlotte sucks even more than I thought.

What do you think?

## Re: BRITNEY SPEARS 2007

---

**Gen Goldman** <GENX1999@gmail.com>
to Ava

Interesting theory immediately disproved by experts in the field.

**11:52 AM EST**

My dad just sent me a Gandhi meme.
Which one?
Be the change you wish to see in the world.
Has my dad never heard that before???
Oh, right. He's been drunk.
Now he's enlightened.
I just LOL'd.
Do I need to respond?
Send back that article about Gandhi's systematic mistreatment of women.
ON IT.

## DR. SHERI BAKER, PH.D.

---

**Ava Helmer** <AVA.HELMER@gmail.com>

to Gen

I just got picked up from college. By my mom. At least she traded in her minivan for a sleek SUV.

I told her about Jake within five seconds of getting in the car. She said, "Wow. Really?" What the fuck is that? I pressed her on it, and she said that we seemed to work well as friends based on the film shoot. She thought he had a thing for Sophia. WHY WOULD A MOTHER SAY THIS TO HER ANXIETY-RIDDEN DAUGHTER? Now I'm going to have to meticulously watch all interactions between them and turn into a jealous lover who abuses animals. (Do you get my reference?? I go to film school now.)

The rest of the ride was not fun. I hate that. I hate that I am my worst self around the two people who are nicest to me. I'm unable to keep my barriers up when I'm around my parents, so all the ugly comes out. Even when I'm mad, I can feel the guilt spreading through my body, but the mad overrides it.

I always apologize once it's passed, but that's not good enough. I'm 18. I can't freak out on my lovely, supportive parents anytime they say something I don't like. I've put them through enough. She literally drove an hour to drive me 20 minutes and then sit in the waiting room while I went into another room and complained about her. I am a terrible person.

The waiting room was nice, though. Very "organized calm." I like when the furniture looks expensive because it means they must have a lot of clients. Or a patron spouse . . .

After 10 minutes of waiting because we were 10 minutes early, Dr. Sheri Baker ushered me into her office. She's middle-aged but dresses extremely well, which is good for me because I'm not above paying someone solely for fashion advice. God knows I need it!

As soon as I sat down, I launched in my rehearsed spiel: how I got sick, when I got sick, in what ways I remain sick. Ava Helmer 101. But Dr. Baker wasn't having it. She said we can get to all of that later. She wanted know how I was doing now. In this moment. This really threw me. I was only emotionally prepared to rehash the past. I have no idea how I'm feeling right now! So instead of being productive and painting my mental health history, I spent forty minutes babbling incoherently about my insecurities as a writer? I alluded to my fear that I will never be hired to write because I have nothing interesting to say, and suddenly we were dissecting a creative-writing workshop I did the summer after freshman year of high school?

This woman asks so many questions. It sucked up the whole session! So now she knows nothing about my current life, other than the fact that I'm a shitty writer, and she has no comprehension of what got me to this very unstable place.

I feel like my mom just wasted $200.

And then to add gas to the fire, I was a complete bitch to my mom on the way home.

## Re: DR. SHERI BAKER, PH.D.

**Gen Goldman** <GENX1999@gmail.com>

to Ava

Awwwww. Poor Ruth. You should send her flowers. I bet she misses me. Her nice daughter.

I'm sorry you feel like the session was a waste of time. But maybe anything you can talk about for 40 minutes is worth talking about for 40 minutes? (Unless it's guys' obsessions with supermodels who would never touch them.)

Why do you think you are a bad writer? I think you are a great writer!

P.S. Molly has reentered my life. She wants to hang out tonight. I'm pretty over watching Shannon eat peanut butter from a jar, so I might go.

P.P.S. Shannon uses her thumb to get the peanut butter. It's fascinating.

**6:30 PM PST**

Speak now or forever hold your peace.

DON'T MARRY JAKE.

hahaha

I'm about to go through initiation.

There is no turning back.

You aren't allowed to drop out???

No I am. I probably will.

OK. Great.

Congratulations?

9:45 PM PST

That was so fucking weird.

What happened? Did you share blood?

I'm legally not allowed to say.

COME ON.

Fine. I'll just assume everyone makes out in white lingerie.

Messy.

Because it's white.

You don't get gay sex.

## ON MOLLY

**Gen Goldman** <GENX1999@gmail.com>

to Ava

Get it? (Diet Coke. Or whatever the code word was.)

To be brief, Molly is still crazy. Perhaps clinically. (Maybe we can get Dr. Baker on Skype for a consult.)

I'm pretty sure she was already drunk when I showed up. Although she denied it and made me take shots with her.

I should have grown suspicious when she insisted on

going to the South End even though all her friends were partying on a roof in the North End. Molly kept saying undergrad parties are lame. She wanted me to meet some of her older friends. People who would really get me and what I'm all about.

It was creepy as fuck. But I was pretty tipsy (because of the forced shots), so I let her lead me there. It took me wayyy too long to realize that we were outside Charlotte's door. Do you know when I realized? When Tom came out. Yes, Tom. That guy I slept with and then mostly ghosted. He was there! To witness Molly's epic meltdown.

He had come outside for a cigarette and spotted me, surprised because he hadn't realized I'd been invited. I HADN'T been invited, by the way. Molly started laughing: "Oh my god, you fucked this guy too, didn't you?" How did she know???? Maybe she has an alcohol-induced sixth sense. Or she was bluffing. Either way, the gloves were off!

She started screaming at me for sleeping with Charlotte. How could I after she had confided in me? She confided in me about a person named CHARLIE . . . but apparently that defense does not hold when you are wasted and mad.

She tried to hit me, Ava. It didn't work because she just swung her arm wildly at my stomach, but she still tried. Tom had to grab her. She then started screaming: "Domestic abuse! My boyfriend is hitting me." Which was, honestly, a pretty smart move. It freaked him out enough to let her go, and then she came charging at me again. I thought she was going to claw me, but instead she started hysterically crying and pulled me into a hug. She then muttered, “We’re nothing to her,” 5 or 6 times. It made me much more uncomfortable than the violence.

I looked up and saw Charlotte peering through the window, but she didn’t come outside. I think that was for the best.

After far more crying than I thought I could physically handle, Molly finally calmed down and asked for ice cream. So we got her ice cream??? The clerk at 7-11 couldn’t help but notice the mascara streaking down her face. Tom paid. What a gentleman. He then escorted us back to the dorms and didn’t even try to kiss me. Which made me invite him in, but he declined. He said I should keep an eye on Molly to make sure she didn’t puke and die.

Really, Tom??

I had no choice but to go to Molly’s room and watch her sleep. At least until I fell asleep . . . I woke up to the sound of Molly shouting at her parents on the phone. Someone had tipped them off (Charlotte??? Tom???) and they were coming to take her home.

By now her roommate was back and willing to take over Molly Watch 2K17. I slipped away and passed out in my own bed.

When I woke up, I went back to Molly’s room, but she was gone. Not just “not there,” but GONE. All her stuff was wiped clean. Her roommate had already pushed the two beds together (lucky bitch).

Now is when I need you to tell me that I didn't cause my friend's psychotic break.

Thanks,
G

**Re: ON MOLLY**

---

**Ava Helmer** <AVA.HELMER@gmail.com>
to Gen

Wow. I'm so sorry. Are you OK? That sounds like a horrible, disturbing night. I can't even imagine what I would do in that situation. Flee? I have no tolerance for physical pain or embarrassment.

This is absolutely, 100% NOT YOUR FAULT. This girl has been extremely troubled since you met her.

If anything, I'm mad at her for sucking you into all of this. I feel like unstable people gravitate toward you (myself included). I want nothing more than for you to make a connection with a normal, boring person who still has good taste in music.

Don't let this upset you any more than it already has. You did nothing wrong (other than fornicating with multiple teachers). And maybe still sleeping with Molly after I said you shouldn't . . .

OK. Maybe you did some stuff wrong. But that's OK. We

all make mistakes, and hopefully she will get the help she needs.

My biggest piece of advice remains: stay clear of Charlotte. That woman attracts drama even more than you. I'm starting to think she is actually the source.

Love you, miss you, wouldn't want to kiss you,

A

**5:32 PM EST**

How do you think any of this is Charlotte's fault?

How do you not?

She didn't even come outside! She just created a mess and left you to deal with it.

She had no idea I knew Molly!

Just like I had no idea she was Charlie.

Or do you not believe that either?

I believe all the things. I just think she isn't taking any responsibility.

And she shouldn't sleep with SO many students.

Wow. One blow job and you're a real expert.

You know my address if you want to mail me an apology for that.

I'm also accepting donations for a better standard of living.

Ask your parents.

**8:21 PM PST**

Are we in a fight?

No.

You're not secretly mad?

No.

OK! Off to lose my v card.

WHAT?? AVA!! WHAT IS HAPPENING!

👋

## WELL PLAYED

---

**Gen Goldman** <GENX1999@gmail.com>

to Ava

I'm officially too curious about your blossoming sexuality to remain annoyed. I hope you are having pleasurable, safe fun. Immediately upon completion, write a steamy letter to *Penthouse* and send it to me instead.

XOXOX MY BABY ANGEL.

## Re: WELL PLAYED

---

**Ava Helmer** <AVA.HELMER@gmail.com>

to Gen

Do my emails read differently now? Now that I'm a full-fledged WOMAN. That's right! I've had a p in my v! On purpose!

Jake went out of his way to make it a special night while still on a budget. He used HotelTonight to get a reservation at a hotel downtown. He borrowed one of his frat brothers' cars and drove us to this loud Italian restaurant. We ordered overpriced food and then I offered to split the bill. He let me, which was maybe good? I said it very softly, but he still took me up on it. Feminism? Who knows.

I packed a huge overnight bag, which Jake mocked the entire time. I'm sorry, but toiletries take up a lot of room. And I can't trust that a hotel blow dryer will have the horsepower needed to adequately dry my hair. He also let me carry my bag. Again. Can't decide if this is good or bad. It wouldn't have mattered if it had wheels, or my OCD allowed me to put it down on the floor while we checked in, but c'est la vie.

The whole check-in process was very uncomfortable. I felt like a little kid who had run away and was trying to buy cigarettes or something. The concierge couldn't have cared less, but I kept waiting for him to ask if we wanted the hourly rate. (GET IT?!)

Once we got in the room, I started to panic talk. About bedbugs. Yep. I started to panic that the hotel had bedbugs. I then announced that I would kill myself if I got bedbugs. Really setting the mood!

Jake didn't talk much. I think he was nervous. He just sat on the bed while I inspected the room for an infestation. It also grossed me out that he sat right on the duvet. Everyone knows you should only touch the parts of a hotel bed that are regularly washed.

After my full failed comedy routine about the minibar (why would anyone pay more for less?), Jake told me to come to the bed. I asked him if we could put the duvet on the floor because of all the bacteria. He laughed and obliged. Then I asked him to take off his clothes because he had already touched the duvet. I think he thought I was being sexy. I wasn't.

He then told me I had to take off my clothes to be fair. I listened even though I still have intense vagina anxiety due to lack of exposure. Is it normal?? Is it disgusting?? Who knows!

Everything happened really quickly after that. Like really quickly. Maybe two minutes of kissing and then he was asking me to put on a condom, which I found confusing because I do not have a penis. By the time I realized he meant put it on HIM, he had already handled the situation.

There was then some struggle upon entrance, but eventually my virginity was taken.

The actual act was "eh." But the aftermath was amazing. He held me all night and we laughed and talked until like 1 AM, which is VERY late for me. I didn't sleep, because how can you possibly sleep when someone is touching you? But it still felt incredible. We got up late and got breakfast at a place down the street. (He paid! It was $13.54.)

He dropped me off at my dorm and said, "See ya later, Girlfriend." I squealed for fifteen minutes. Jessica had to leave the room.

Anyway, the whole thing was super worth it because you're not secretly mad at me anymore! Who knew all I needed to do was put out!

## Re: WELL PLAYED

---

**Gen Goldman** <GENX1999@gmail.com>

to Ava

IT'S LIT FAM! My baby girl is a woman in heteronormative culture! She's out there proving penetration is overrated!

Proud of you, boo. Don't tell your parents.

ALSO: SHOP K-Y LUBRICANTS ON PRIME PANTRY.

**3:21 PM PST**

I haven't heard from Jake. What if this was all an elaborate scheme to take my virginity and he has fled the country?

Why would he flee the country?

Commitment to scam.

Do you think he could not find a single other person to have nonscam sex with?

I have no idea! I've never had nonscam sex!

I feel the need to tell you that it's only been 3 hours.

3 hours is a real trigger time for you.

I feel like a dirty slut who is being punished for having premarital sex.

. . .

Delete that. Obviously.

I think you are spiraling.

Absolutely.

Can you go distract yourself?

Or maybe just text him?

It's 2017. Not 2038. I'll text him first if I'm pregnant.

Don't be ridiculous. You don't have to contact someone just because you're getting an abortion.

That's like sending a card for Arbor Day.

I'm so glad I have you to put everything in perspective.

What are you going to do?

I have to go look at a cut of the short with Curtis.

No better way to get over my ex-boyfriend than to stare at his face all afternoon.

#Hollywood

#VIPLYFESTYLE

#ISHARRYSTYLESBI?

He's not bi. You have to get over this.

## SQUAD GOALS

---

**Gen Goldman** <GENX1999@gmail.com>

to Ava

I made a friend. That's right. A friend who I have no interest in sleeping with. (I guess Kent is my friend. But he is my editor first and foremost.)

We all went to Kent, my editor's, house for a kick back. Every department came because there was free cake. (One of the managing editors has a hookup at this bakery. Cannot stress enough the importance of having someone in your life who has a hookup to a bakery.)

Alex was there. He was a brat the whole night. I mean he laughed and mingled and had a good time but wouldn't look at me once. Even though I looked incredible and had the best party stories.

But I didn't care because I finally talked to the 2 girls from the Lifestyle section. One of them, Kelly, is about as basic as Emerson admits. Jazmin on the other hand is cool as fuck. She's from Miami and does not give a shit. She has a popular fashion Tumblr and more bandeaus than you can even imagine.

She's a junior, and last year her friend (now graduated) made this crazy drink at the *Beacon* holiday party. It's called The Force. You need to make it in a bathtub.

So we made it in the bathtub. Kent, my editor, was upset at first, but then the Force was with him and he got over it REAL QUICK. We were the hits of the party. Sitting on the edge of the tub, using a ladle to get turnt.

Turns out you can get to know someone real fast when you're wasted. I feel closer to Jazmin than anyone else on this coast and we had barely talked before last night. She is just a good person disguised as a cool person. You would love her. We're going to get brunch in 15. I'm brunching! What am I? Well-adjusted and straight?!

Did that jerkface ever text you? Or is he still air ballooning around the world?

## Re: SQUAD GOALS

**Ava Helmer** <AVA.HELMER@gmail.com>

to Gen

Are you trying to break my heart, Gen? I mean I'm glad you have a friend or whatever, but it seems like you're moving really fast. It took six months for you to even eat breakfast near me.

I'll try to be the bigger person here, ignore your new friendship, and change the topic to make it about me.

I spent four hours with Curtis yesterday. His first cut was . . . questionable? It ran like 15 minutes. The script was 7 pages. LOTS of reaction shots.

I might need to work on my poker face for disappointment.

I made a few audible "ughs," which was not nice to Curtis. I tried to cover it up later, and we reached a really good middle ground. (The cut is still over 6, but change takes time.)

Sophia did a great job. Jake . . . not so much. Most of the editing involved looking for alternate takes of Jake not overacting. We ended up using a lot of his face before I called, "Action."

He finally texted me, by the way. To ask if I was sore. GROSS! SO GROSS! I wasn't, but I wrote back yes to be nice. I told him I was editing, and he got kind of mad that he wasn't invited. I didn't think he would want to be in the editing session. Also, it's not like I gave him approval over the edit or something, which I probably should have given to my parents.

I sent him a link to the short after the edit as a courtesy, and then he emailed me back a whole slew of notes. Um. Do I have to listen to these notes? Most of them are bad. I guess a couple make sense . . . I don't like being criticized. Not really a turn-on for me.

Wow. I'm so mad about the notes I actually forgot you are replacing me with your new bandeau-wearing BFF. At least remember me whenever you get ice cream. I love ice cream.

**10:34 PM EST**

I want to see the short!

No! It's not ready!

But you sent it to stupid Jake!

I love you more in a single second than he'll love anyone in his entire lifetime!

Awww, that's so mean and creepy.

So you will send?

No. My fragile ego can't afford any more notes.

I'll be a yes-woman! I'll love it all!

That's even worse!

## ADULT EMANCIPATION

**Gen Goldman** <GENX1999@gmail.com>

to Ava

Can you emancipate when you are over 18? Just to send a strong message that you don't want to hear from your family anymore.

I made the horrible mistake of disclosing Molly's departure to my parents. My father started rambling about addiction and releasing one's self from one's ego. He then asked me if I've taken responsibility for enabling her. WTF? I'm not her drug dealer. Apparently my energy encourages reckless behavior. Really, Dad? Do you think Ava is reckless? (He finds you to be too caught up in your "sickness" to be tempted by other vices.)

Within a minute I was screaming: Did Mom enable you?

Is that why you've been checked out for 20 years? He didn't take my bait and remained eerily calm.

I hate people who remain calm. It makes my shouting less satisfying.

My mom finally butted in and told him to leave me alone. She then immediately ruined this act of solidarity by taking complete responsibility for my dad's inability to stay sober.

Again. WTF? How can my mom possibly think it's all her fault? How can he let her think that? Their entire dynamic is disgusting. Hope started crying before I could hang up the phone, so they hung up on me. I can't believe they got to keep all the power AGAIN.

I'm not an enabler, am I? Do you think I act like my mom? Am I the reason Molly left?

I'm raging out.

## Re: ADULT EMANCIPATION

---

**Ava Helmer** <AVA.HELMER@gmail.com>

to Gen

Jesus Christ. I don't think you can get emancipated as an adult, but maybe my parents can still legally adopt you?

I wish you recorded these conversations so you could

use them as ammo in the future. Or just put them in a documentary about crazy people.

You are not an enabler. You are a college kid who sometimes makes bad decisions. You're not responsible for some random girl's life. She was screwed up before you even entered the picture. The only thing I wish would change *maybe* is the kind of people you surround yourself with. You don't need to hang out with uptight losers (present company excluded), but maybe there is a happy medium?

Either way, that's just something to think about in the future. In the meantime, I suggest putting your dad's face on a dartboard and really going to town.

**7:12 AM PST**

I think I have bedbugs.

U don't have bedbugs.

HOW COULD YOU POSSIBLY KNOW THAT?

Sixth sense.

*Bug sense.

This isn't funny.

I should have never have gone to the hotel.

Yeah, u totally should have lost it in that frat house.

My whole body is itchy.

Do you have bite marks?

I have mystery bumps.

Those are just boobs.

( . ) ( . )

## EXTRA! EXTRA! READ ALL ABOUT IT!

**Gen Goldman** <GENX1999@gmail.com>

to Ava

Your favorite lady's got another hit on her hands! That's right! Our scathing exposé is going viral! On a campus of under 4,000 people.

There are already rumors of a student protest. I'm not sure what their angle will be exactly, but I can't wait to cover it!

I think the good news put a cease-fire on my feud with Alex. We exchanged a smile and a few words. I thought about asking for a high five but didn't want to push it.

I'm a little afraid I'm going to get spoiled by all of this critical acclaim. I wonder how Kent, my editor, is going to feel when I become his editor in chief.

Charlotte reached out about it, obviously. She wants to celebrate. I'm gonna tell her to invite Tom so we can turn this into a real party.

JK. I will probably just go to dinner with Jazmin. I've become very boring in my success.

**2:15 PM PST**

My mom just sent me your article.

Hahaha

Does she think she keeps better tabs on you than me?

I mean we do FaceTime all the time.

No you don't.

Do you??

💁

## IMPOSTOR SYNDROME

---

**Ava Helmer** <AVA.HELMER@gmail.com>

to Gen

Remember when I first told you I was going to join a sorority and you pretended like that was a good idea but we both knew you were lying?

Tonight was Monday Night Dinner. (A terrible tradition wherein I have to get dressed up every Monday and eat cooked carrots with the entire house.) I entered the room and looked for an open seat. All of these girls are supposed to be my closest friends and confidantes, but the idea of talking to them made me more nervous than asking a stranger to push a floor number on an elevator. I feel like no one here genuinely likes me and they are all forming these friendships while I sit around looking like a moron. No one is rude or anything. It's worse. It's like I'm not even there. It's how I felt every moment of high school when you weren't around. When am I going to outgrow this feeling? When will I find my people? Grad school? Nursing home?

I finally picked a spot next to Chelsea, who I thought was becoming my friend but then stopped trying a couple weeks ago. (If you'll remember, she was too busy sucking face at a party to accompany me to the bathroom that one time.) She smiled and everything but spent the whole dinner talking to everyone else. I think I maybe said 10 words, and you know how hard it is to get me to shut up.

Emma was my only real friend here and now she's gone.

You think I would be better at all of this since I went to that social skills class when I was 12. I wonder if it is too late to get a refund.

Our Date Dash with ZBT is coming up. (It's just a big party with my sorority and Jake's fraternity.) Maybe that will be fun? Or awful.

I wish I liked to drink. Drunk people seem happier.

## Re: IMPOSTOR SYNDROME

---

**Gen Goldman** <GENX1999@gmail.com>

to Ava

As a child of an alcoholic, let me assure you that drunk people are absolutely much happier. And destructive and unhealthy and miserable! You don't need to be intoxicated to have fun. You just need more stimulation than a room full of crop tops talking about *The Bachelor.*

I never thought you shouldn't join a sorority. I thought you should *try* to join a sorority and see how it went. It sounds like it's not going great? What's your reasoning for staying in it at this point?

I don't want to suggest a pro-and-con list, but if you decided to do something that dorky on your own, I wouldn't be against it.

## Re: IMPOSTOR SYNDROME

**Ava Helmer** <AVA.HELMER@gmail.com>

to Gen

**PROS**

1) Normalcy. After a childhood of mostly hanging out with my parents and attending cognitive behavioral therapy sessions, being in a sorority feels excitingly average. It's what regular, evenly balanced people do before getting married and having kids without the fear of postpartum depression.

2) Cool. I feel cool. Even if it's not a top house, some girls don't get into any house. And I got in. So I want to rub that in people's faces a bit.

3) Social life. I attend class for maybe a total of 15 hours 4 days a week. I need set activities to fill the rest of the time. Outside of the house I really only have Sophia and Emma, who have their own set of friends. I guess I could

try to transition into one of their crews, but that seems forced and uncomfortable. The rest of the screenwriting kids hang out a lot. Maybe I should attend more of their events, even though they make fun of my lack of film knowledge.

4) Boys. I know I already have a boyfriend, but what if we break up and I need to find a new one? Drunk frat guys seem like low-hanging fruit.

**CONS**

1) I hate it.

Technically, pros are winning in terms of numbers . . .

12:04 AM EST

You have to quit the sorority.

I know.

## MY SEPTUM AND OTHER UPDATES

**Gen Goldman** <GENX1999@gmail.com>

to Ava

I'm officially in love with Jazmin. And not sexually! If anything, I keep waiting to fall sexually in love with her, but our sisterhood bond is too strong. (The body rejects incest. That is just science.)

We spent all afternoon and night together and I didn't get bored once! That is huge for me when not sleeping with someone. She cooked us dinner??? Yes. I had a home-cooked meal that did not start in a can or microwavable box. I didn't know vegetables could taste edible! Maybe I will not die at 27 now like all of the greats.

Her apartment is rad. She has a studio in the North End. Her boyfriend used to live with her but now he lives back in Miami. They're in an open relationship. I didn't realize straight people could be so chill too.

After we got red wine tipsy, we wanted to go do something fun that didn't involve other people, so we went to this tattoo parlor. Jazmin got a heart on her finger and I got a septum piercing. NBD. Just the coolest piercing a chick can get other than her nipple. I'm about to post 10 different photos to my Insta. I already know you will hate it, but I'm obsessed. I look like a bull. In a very good sexy in-charge way.

I wanted Jazmin to get her septum pierced too, but she said too many people already think she's gay.

Ava. I look like a boss. Can't wait for my parents to not notice.

**9:32 AM PST**

I love it!!!

Really??

Oh, yeah! It looks amazing!

I think I should get one too.
Ya?
Definitely! After I get a few teardrop face tattoos.
That's not an OK joke.
Why???
For so many social, economic, and racial reasons.
Sorry

## MILEY & LIAM

---

**Ava Helmer** <AVA.HELMER@gmail.com>
to Gen

Remember when Miley and Liam broke up and everyone thought that it was over forever but then OUT OF NOWHERE they got back together stronger than ever!?? I remember. I think about it every day. Especially on this day of all days where I called my brand-new boyfriend an "assjerk."

I feel like I haven't set the scene for you in a while. So let me do so now.

INT. ZBT HOUSE—JAKE'S ROOM—EVENING

The air is warm from a series of elaborate Snapchat videos wherein Tyler drenched himself with Gatorade while sitting on his bed.

Tyler exits to shower. Leaving Jake and Ava alone for the first time.

AVA
He just ruined his bed.

JAKE
Nah. It will dry.

AVA
He's not going to wash it???

JAKE
He'll wash it or it will dry. Whatever. It's not our bed.

Jake tries to make a move on Ava, but she is too antsy.

AVA
I think I'm gonna quit Gamma Phi.

Jake laughs. Distracted by his attempt to make another move.

AVA
I'm serious. I hate it.

JAKE
Since when?

AVA
Since always.

A bit of debate wherein Ava concedes she hasn't always hated it. The first week was pretty fun. But that's it.

JAKE
I don't think you should quit. Our Date Dash is next week! We'll have fun!

AVA
OK. I'll quit next week.

JAKE
No! Just give it the semester.

AVA
Why do you care if I'm in a sorority?

JAKE
It's more fun. It's a similar lifestyle. We won't see each other as much if you drop out.

AVA
Why? It's not like we are in the same sorority.

Jake shrugs and becomes angry quiet.

AVA
I don't feel like I fit in.

JAKE
That's because you're not trying.

Welcome to the climax of our argument where I find out that Jake thinks I purposefully stay on the sidelines of social events because I'm "better" than everyone. EVER HEARD OF SOCIAL ANXIETY, JAKE? Or were you not listening when I gave you a complete breakdown of my various disorders.

I cry. Then yell. Then cry some more. He shuts down. I apologize. He thinks I've changed my mind about staying in the sorority and tries to make another move. I clarify that I'm apologizing for the yelling and crying. Not for my informed decision to quit the sorority. He gets mad again. I ask if I should leave. He shrugs. I leave.

Red Gatorade drips onto the floor.

I don't get it. Why does it matter if I stay?? I understand the Date Dash thing and I'm willing to wait that out, but four years of not knowing where to sit on a Monday night? No guy is worth that. Maybe Michael B. Jordan. But that's it.

**11:52 AM EST**

Ew. Ew. Ew.
Dump him!
What? No! It was one fight.
But he's trying to control you!
He's not. I think he was just surprised.
I don't care what he was. He should never tell you what to do.
I tell you what to do all the time and you don't dump me.
Ur not a cis straight male.
Try to remember that you've only been gay for two minutes.

I've been gay my whole life.

I thought you didn't believe in labels.

I'm simplifying it for you.

Got it. Well, I'll go live my dumb straight lifestyle with my controlling boyfriend.

Remember to shave your legs and adhere to unnatural beauty standards!

## IF AT FIRST YOU DON'T SUCCEED...

---

**Gen Goldman** <GENX1999@gmail.com>
to Ava

Drop the class. Unfortunately, it is too late for me to drop Earth Science: Natural Disasters, so I will have to settle for a D-. I don't understand why the honors program requires science. This is a vocational and technical school. Everyone here already knows what they want to do. And it's not digging up rocks.

My professor had no empathy. I asked if I could retake the exam since I've been absorbed in the paper, and he was like: nah. So now my honors scholarship might be on probation, and there is no way I can afford to go here without it. My dead grandma's government bonds aren't enough to cover the whole tuition.

I'm so fucked. I guess I'll have to actually study for the final. Remember when being exceptionally smart was enough to get by?

## Re: IF AT FIRST YOU DON'T SUCCEED...

**Ava Helmer** <AVA.HELMER@gmail.com>

to Gen

Oh, no! I'm so sorry! What happened? Did you just not study at all? You're the smartest person I know, but there's no way for you to know details about Earth's geological core without actually reading about it.

Could you do extra credit of some sort? Does that exist in college?

I'm sure it will be fine. Just start trying and ace the final. The scholarship is there until it isn't, so there is no use worrying about something that isn't actually happening. (This is a Dr. Baker original! I'm loving it!)

If it makes you feel any better, I showed my parents the most recent cut of my short and they both smiled and said, "It's not really for us." I cried.

**9:13 PM EST**

Why does everyone get to see this motherfucking movie other than me?

No one else is going to see it. Ever.

Come on. Did they really say that?

Basically! They didn't laugh the entire time, and when I asked if they hated it, my mom said, "I was just trying to listen."

Ruth has a hard time hearing!

It's awful. I can't believe I wasted everyone's time making it.

It's not awful. U've never done anything awful.

What about my wardrobe all of 10th grade?

Not the same. And it was worth it for the TBT photos.

I feel so embarrassed! I'm such an idiot!

UR not an idiot. I'm actually failing a class and I'm not embarrassed. I'm just mad.

You're always mad.

Correct.

## YOU WERE RIGHT

---

**Gen Goldman** <GENX1999@gmail.com>

to Ava

Revel in it. Brag about it. And then shut up please.

I spent the night with Alex. WE DIDN'T HAVE SEX. But we did kiss for a bit!! EEP!

How did this happen, you ask? I have no idea.

I went into the office last night to pitch some ideas to Kent, my editor, but he was off LARPing somewhere. The only other person around was Alex. But he wasn't working. He was just watching *Curb* on the managing editor's computer and eating popcorn. I didn't even know the *Beacon* had a microwave. I pulled up a chair and we didn't speak for an entire episode. But by the third one we were having a great time and the popcorn was gone. He asked if I wanted to get a real meal and discuss Larry David's dependence on J. B. Smoove. I agreed. I thought we would just go somewhere local, but he suggested this poke place in East Boston.

We took the Blue Line to get there. I fell into him on the T and then sort of stayed close. As an experiment. He didn't move away. He was wearing a bow tie and hair gel. It almost felt like we hadn't been involved in a feud since the moment we met!

Dinner was fun. I felt nervous for some reason. In addition to being a snarky asshole, Alex is very smart. I don't feel dumb around him, but I certainly feel silly if I talk too long or monopolize the conversation (my normal MO).

After dinner he asked if I had plans. I said I didn't and he looked surprised. He said he assumed I always had plans. For some reason I found this offensive and felt the need to inform him that I often do nothing and that my best friend in the entire world is a huge homebody weirdo. He laughed and asked if I wanted to go home now. I said no. So we went candlepin bowling.

Turns out, it's even harder to bowl when the pins are smaller. But that didn't stop Alex from crushing it. He was like exceptionally good at using a heavy ball to knock down wood. I don't know why this is so attractive to me.

At this point I still couldn't tell if it was a date or not, and I think Alex felt the same way. I tried to make it a point to ask him to show me how to throw the ball correctly, but he just talked through his own throw instead of showing me with my body. WHICH IS THE MOST CLASSIC DATE MOVE.

We finished a third round around 11 and then stood in front of the train station not sure what to do. My mind was racing with all of these thoughts, and then I heard your voice loud and clear: "He likes you, you idiot!" So I kissed him.

And it was ALL THE FEELS. Like the MOST FEELS! My stomach turned and it was romantic. I felt like a princess? Or a knight? Holy shit, was it good. I didn't even want to get a room. I just wanted to stand outside with him forever.

WHO AM I?! THIS IS DISGUSTING!

Finally I asked if I could come home with him, and he looked startled. He always looks startled whenever I say anything. He mumbled, "Sure," took my hand, and led me to the train.

I don't think I said anything the entire way home. And I was completely awake. Is this how shy people feel all the time? It's horrible. And exhausting. I kept trying to think of something interesting or informed to say. I came up with nothing. Alex didn't say anything either, but he seemed content to sit in silence, which is another type of person I can't relate to. It took all of my restraint to stop myself from taking out my phone and playing Best Fiends. Alex seems too intellectual for a puzzle adventure game.

Once we got to his house, I felt more comfortable. We

started joking about Kent, my editor, who is always a source of endless fodder. Who is picking out his clothes? Why do they not fit?

After a full hour of not kissing, I asked if we could kiss again. Alex laughed. I had to ask a SECOND time. He allowed it. We then did some PG bed kissing until I fell asleep (I'm assuming from all of the emotional exhaustion). In the morning, he told me not to tell anyone.

Yes, you heard that right. HE told ME, the master of discretion, not to tell anyone. Who am I going to tell? Kent the virgin?

He then mumbled some stuff about work and not wanting to mix business with pleasure. I honestly stopped listening because I was so offended. Did he really think I was going to tell anyone? Why would I do that? We are both vying for the same position. I'm not giving the *Beacon* any ammo to use against me.

Honestly, the whole thing felt like a power play, but I'm going to ignore it. Maybe he has some secret girlfriend. Maybe he finds my unrelenting confidence embarrassing? Either way, this will be a secret, torrid affair.

How was your night?

HUGS AND MANIPULATION,
G

## Re: YOU WERE RIGHT

**Ava Helmer** <AVA.HELMER@gmail.com>
to Gen

How have you hooked up with so many people in so little amount of time? This is not judgment. This is pure admiration and genuine curiosity. How. Do. You. Do. It?? Is it a pheromone? Is it something to be taught? Have you just been lying this whole time and you're a virgin? TELL ME.

I also have some gender and sexuality questions about Alex's . . . hardware. But I am afraid to ask. Maybe you could just tell me and not make me feel like an ignorant IDIOT.

I had an uneventful night writing. I don't know if I've mentioned this before, but I HATE WRITING. It is the worst, most painful exercise in masochism. Who am I to think that I have anything worth saying? All of my assignments have been trite and predictable. How will I possibly write an entire feature next semester? (Technically I only have to write an entire outline, but it's basically the same thing minus 80 pages.) I would change majors, but I can't think of anything else worth doing (you know, other than saving lives or making a lot of money).

I know this is dumb, but I *feel* like a writer? Even if I hate writing? Is that allowed?

Meeting with Curtis today to finish the cut. I want to scrap the whole thing, but that doesn't seem fair to everyone who worked on it for free. I should probably have a cast and crew screening. Maybe on the night of the ZBT Date Dash???? Jokes.

I hate everything.

**10:27 AM EST**

Why does my body hurt all the time?

Hmmm

Poor diet? Lack of exercise? The human condition?

Cool. Cool. Any tips?

Other than murder-suicide.

Drink more water?

REALISTIC TIPS! SOMETHING I COULD ACTUALLY DO!

When having sex, try more vigorous positions to increase your heart rate.

THANK YOU! V HELPFUL.

I can't believe you've had sex.

I know it's crazy!

What positions have you tried?

Just the one.

## REAL HOUSEWIVES OF USC

**Ava Helmer** <AVA.HELMER@gmail.com>

to Gen

Sorry. That was the best I could do in terms of a subject line about female drama. I guess it's not even female drama. Maybe I should I have said BACHELOR IN USC. (Is it clear that I don't watch reality TV and have a hard time connecting with my peers?)

I had lunch with Sophia and started talking to her about the short and referred to Jake as my boyfriend. She made a face. I guess she didn't know we were back together or official. I was confused because I thought she liked Jake. Maybe a little too much. It turns out that she did like Jake until he tried to kiss her in my parents' house during a "take five."

Apparently she found the come-on aggressive, and he got pissy when she rejected him. I listened to her story in complete shock. On the one hand, we weren't together at the time and he was allowed to make a fool of himself however and with whomever he wanted. On the OTHER hand, what the fuck! He tried to hook up with another girl in my house??? Why is he dating me if he doesn't even like me as much as he likes Sophia? Am I sloppy seconds? But not even sloppy, because she rejected him? Also, why did she reject him? Was it out of loyalty to me or an aversion to him? Is there anyone I can trust anymore?

I don't know what to do. We are supposed to hang out

tonight, but I am so mad and anxious I want to rip my skin off. Why can't anything ever just be nice or easy? Why am I in a constant state of torment? If this is life, no thanks.

**10:01 PM EST**

Are you hurting yourself?

Ava?

I'm gonna call your mom if you don't respond.

**9:05 PM PST**

Sorry. Was in class.

Only you would go to class during a complete meltdown.

I have to go. You are required to go to class.

Did you hurt yourself?

Not bad. Just scratches.

Where?

Stomach. It's fine. No razor.

Are you gonna tell your mom?

No way. Maybe my therapist.

OK.

No boy is worth this.

It's not his fault. It's my fault. I don't have coping mechanisms.

OK. Can you ask for those?

Ha. I've been asking my whole life.

What are you going to do now?

See my cheating boyfriend.

Don't. Cancel until you feel better.

I will never feel better.

That's the spirit! ♥ ♥

**12:32 AM EST**

How is it going?

I don't know.

How do you not know?

I don't know.

Do you want me to talk to him?

No.

**9:40 PM PST**

Stop FaceTiming me!

I want to talk to Jake!

You're drunk. Go home.

Jazmin thinks you should dump him.

You're both drunk.

Jazmin wants to talk to Jake!

Power off.

**WHAT THE FUCK HAPPENED?**

---

**Gen Goldman** <GENX1999@gmail.com>

to Ava

**Re: WHAT THE FUCK HAPPENED?**

---

**Ava Helmer** <AVA.HELMER@gmail.com>

to Gen

I don't want to tell you.

**Re: WHAT THE FUCK HAPPENED?**

---

**Gen Goldman** <GENX1999@gmail.com>

to Ava

Why?? Are you OK??

**Re: WHAT THE FUCK HAPPENED?**

---

**Ava Helmer** <AVA.HELMER@gmail.com>

to Gen

I'm fine. I'm better. I just know you won't like what happened so I don't want to talk about it.

## Re: WHAT THE FUCK HAPPENED?

**Gen Goldman** <GENX1999@gmail.com>

to Ava

“That’s not how friendship works.”—Ava Helmer, 2014, 2015, 2016, 2017

I don’t care “what” happened. I just care if you’re OK.

## Re: WHAT THE FUCK HAPPENED?

**Ava Helmer** <AVA.HELMER@gmail.com>

to Gen

I’m fine. I talked to Jake about it, and he thought I already knew. He assumed girls tell each other everything and thought it was water under the bridge. He never really liked her; he just got caught up in the shoot. (Once we wrapped he realized that she is a bit of a bitch. I don’t think that’s true, but she is standoffish.) If anything, the incident with her made him realize how much he liked me. We also talked about the sorority, and now I understand his point of view better. He wants to have fun with me and spend more time with me and thinks it will be easier if we are both in the Greek system. I told him I’d go to Date Dash with an open mind and not make any rash decisions right away. He felt terrible that I felt terrible and stroked my hair for the longest anyone has stroked my hair. I don't know. I want to be happy. And he (mostly) makes me happy. Don't judge me.

**11:56 PM EST**

OK. Love you.

You don't think I'm an idiot?

Don't put words in my mouth.

## AND THE PLOT THICKENS

---

**Gen Goldman** <GENX1999@gmail.com>

to Ava

Last night at our weekly meeting, Kent, my editor, announced that our faculty adviser, Ric, would be stepping down due to a family obligation in the Midwest. First of all, that's weird. And vague. Don't tell a bunch of nosey reporters that. Now we are all trying to figure out what's wrong with his mysterious Midwestern family and why he would leave a great job at the *Globe* to figure it out. (My theory involves a second, secret family and a love child.)

In the meantime we've been assigned an interim adviser and that person is, drumroll, please, my old friend Charlotte Huang. So now I've had sex with my TA and my faculty adviser. Pretty cool.

Not everyone was pleased with this news. And by

everyone, I mean Alex. He actually left the room after Kent announced it. I think I was the only one who noticed because I was the only one who had been obsessively monitoring his every adorable move. After people were given their assignments, the meeting ended and I found Alex typing furiously in the hallway. I informed him that he had been assigned a riveting piece about the new key cards for the dorms. He wouldn't even look at me.

After a minute of silence he finally growled, "I'm not going to work for someone who is openly transphobic." Yikes! How do you argue with that? Also, do I want to argue with that when he is my biggest competition? If he walks away, that staff spot is mine. This is not a great thing to think, but I thought it. And I also felt embarrassed because I'm not trans so I have no idea what it's like to feel attacked and unsafe.

"It's only temporary." Not the right response. Alex launched into a tirade about allowing bad behavior to continue and not standing up to things because "it's not that big a deal." In my defense, I didn't realize the extent of Charlotte's transphobia. Alex showed me an article she wrote about female safe spaces, and it was . . . questionable. She didn't directly use the term "women-born-women," but it was certainly implied.

After I picked my jaw up from the floor, I told Alex to talk to Kent. Maybe they could get someone else. It's only an interim position, it's not like it was formally announced outside of our meeting. But he wouldn't. He doesn't want to look like a crybaby tattletale. He would rather make a statement and leave. Maybe write an exposé about it for *em Magazine* (our biggest/only competition).

I thought this was a dumb strategy. So I flagged down Kent and showed him Charlotte's article. Kent replied, "Aren't you dating Charlotte?" WHOA KENT!! How does he know?? Also, who says "dating"???

I quickly replied no, but not before Alex turned a shade of purple I have never seen in nature before. Was it anger? Embarrassment? Jealously? A familiar desire to throttle Kent?

Kent promised he would look into it and talk to the managing editors and editor in chief (I always forget that he's not actually in charge because he has such a commanding presence in his itty-bitty T-shirts.) I thanked him. Alex grunted.

Kent then went off to do whatever Kent does (which I'm starting to think is NSA-level spying). I asked Alex if he wanted to keep talking somewhere else. He said no.

I wish I could elaborate, but he literally just said "no" and left. WTF? I didn't write transphobic articles, Alex! Why are you mad at me?? Men be cray cray.

## Re: AND THE PLOT THICKENS

---

**Ava Helmer** <AVA.HELMER@gmail.com>

to Gen

Here is another cray-cray thought. Maybe extensively Google everyone's online profile before having sex with them? Did you really not know Charlotte was problematic? Please tell me that you're finally done with her.

10:05 AM EST

For someone who asks not to be judged, you certainly fling around a lot of judgment.

Jake isn't openly transphobic.

How do you know? It's not like ur super enlightened to that stuff.

???

You asked me about Alex's genitals.

Privately!!!

Still.

OH, SO I CAN'T ASK ANY QUESTIONS?

That seems like a GREAT way to stay informed.

It's not a thing you're allowed to ask.

WELL, NOW I KNOW.

And I'm embarrassed.

I'm done with Charlotte.

Sure.

3:25 PM PST

Did you talk to my mom?

Y?

So you talked to her?

Yeah. She checks in. I'm the daughter she never had.

Did you tell her I've been hurting myself?

No . . .

GEN! It was a couple of scratches. Now she wants me to move home!

What?! I told her it wasn't a big deal.

Then why did you bring it up???

Just to monitor it. I'm so far away I feel helpless.

I just don't want a repeat of junior year.

Well, there is a higher chance of that now that my parents are going to ruin my life.

Can you talk to them? I'm sure they're just overreacting and will calm down.

Yeah, my parents are so calm and rational when it comes to my mental health.

I'm sorry. Do you want me to call her back?

No. You've done enough.

**5:21 PM PST**

They said I could stay.

Really?? That's great!

Yeah. But if I do it again, I'm out of the dorm.

Are you going to do it again?

You guys don't get it. It's just a coping mechanism. If I wanted to actually kill myself, I would just kill myself.

What a great case for self-harm! Does it need a spokesperson?

I don't want to talk to you anymore.

OK. Sorry for caring!

## TO BE, OR NOT TO BE

---

**Gen Goldman** <GENX1999@gmail.com>

to Ava

Dana Scully for Halloween? Or maybe Sia? I could just wear a blanket over my face? There are so many choices and so many articles:

25 FEMINIST COSTUMES FOR THIS HALLOWEEN

14 BADASS LADIES TO BE THIS HOLIDAY SEASON

32 REASONS NOT TO SLUT SHAME ON HALLOWEEN

Part of me wants to go as my little sister and then when people ask me what I am I can say "a mistake." JUST KIDDING. They love her more than me.

What are you going to be, my little angel princess?

SKULLS AND PUMPKINS,
G

## Re: TO BE, OR NOT TO BE

**Ava Helmer** <AVA.HELMER@gmail.com>

to Gen

This year for Halloween, I think I will be: mortified. It's sort of an abstract idea, but I can pull it off.

The Gamma Phi/ZBT Date Dash was last night. I can safely say it will be my last Gamma Phi event unless I am reincarnated as a cooler person.

Everything started out fine because Jake was there. I didn't have to worry about where to sit on the bus because I sat next to him. I didn't have to worry about where to go because I went with him. I felt very safe and cared for.

But then Jake got drunk. And drunk Jake isn't great at staying put. I quickly lost track of him and found myself standing by myself even though it was an event for my sorority. Everyone around me was wasted, but I only managed to take one shot before feeling like I was going to vomit. I finally found Jake making an ass of himself on the dance floor.

I tried to get him to sit down with me, but he wouldn't. He said I could dance or I could leave. So I left. The event. Which you are not supposed to do. But I couldn't take it anymore, so I Ubered home. (This is completely against the rules, just to give you some insight into my mental state.)

I stayed awake until 1 AM waiting for Jake to call me in a panic, but he never did. I'm sending in my resignation now. At least Emma is happy for me. Or I hope she'll be happy for me when I tell her.

**11:54 AM EST**

Please tell me you are going to dump him.

If he ever bothers to reach out. Maybe he forgot he has a girlfriend.

He certainty acted like it.

I can't wait for you to meet someone who loves you like I do.

As a platonic friend?

Funny.

I'm sorry he is a douche.

Did you officially quit?

Yeah, but no one wrote back.

Maybe they all forgot I was in the sorority.

Who is this again?

JOKES. I could never forget you.

Eh. I give it another year.

Jazmin sounds pretty cool.

Yeah. Too cool. I prefer to be the cool one in the relationship.

In that case: BFF 4 LYFE.

## SPORTY SHANNON

---

**Gen Goldman** <GENX1999@gmail.com>

to Ava

In an effort to continue my study of Shannon, I accepted her invitation to watch a Quidditch match. Unfortunately for me there was little magic to be found. There was, however, a shitload of unabashed geekiness.

What follows geekiness around? Why, Kent, my editor, of course! Turns out, that guy moonlights as the official announcer for all Boston-area Quidditch games! He's actually pretty funny, and I saw not 1 but 3 living females swoon over him. No wonder that guy has so much awkward swagger!

Shannon is just a sub on the Boylston Berserkers, but that didn't stop her from shouting THE ENTIRE TIME. That girl has a mouth on her! She trashed-talked the Old North Outlaws from start to finish, and if anyone other than me had been listening, I'm sure some sort of broomstick brawl would have broken out. Both Jazmin and I were riveted.

I wish I could tell you who won, but I was too caught up in Kent's radioworthy commentary as well as Shannon's repressed rage.

You may be asking yourself: Why would anyone bother to play a made-up game? Couldn't tell you! Probably involves a limited high school social life and Emerson's lack of actual sports. The entire day felt decidedly British, which was a nice cheap way to feel cultured.

I would give Quidditch 4 out of 5 stars. (1 star deducted because the brooms don't actually fly.)

Next up: observing Shannon's beauty routine without her consent.

How you doing, boo?

## ALL THE SINGLE LADIES

**Ava Helmer** <AVA.HELMER@gmail.com>

to Gen

It's official. I now have an ex-boyfriend. After not hearing from Jake all day, he finally texted me this: "Just woke up. Had a lot (of booze) to sleep off."

WHAT??? Did he really not notice that I had LEFT? How is that possible?? So I wrote back: "We need to talk." He wrote back: "Y?" Off to a great start!

Within an hour I was in his room crying and pleading with him not to break up with me even though I had gone there to break up with him! I don't really know how this happened. I guess I expected some resistance or pleading, but instead he replied, "I've been thinking the same thing." FUCK YOU! Since when???

This response freaked me out so much I was desperate to fix it. I can barely emotionally handle dumping someone. I definitely can't handle being dumped. It didn't matter, though. He was completely checked out.

After it became clear he wasn't going to change his mind, I stormed out shouting, "Let me know if you want Sophia's number!" He murmured, "I already have it."

REMIND ME TO NEVER DATE AGAIN! FEELINGS ARE TERRIBLE! PEOPLE ARE TERRIBLE.

Maybe I will move home.

**12:17 PM EST**

Don't move home.

Why not? My parents are the only people on this coast who like me.

What about Sophia? What about Emma?

What about them? I never see them.

What about Curtis?

He has a girlfriend!

As a friend!

I've yelled at him too much for him to be my friend.

I'm still your friend! And you yell at me all the time!

I do???

Of course no one likes me.

Call Emma. Make her hang out.

That's embarrassing.

Yes. Asking someone to hang out = very embarrassing.

You just ask random people to hang out??

All the time. I haven't spent a moment alone in years.

Maybe I will transfer to Emerson.

We would love to have you!

**REMEMBER WHEN ZAYN LEFT ONE DIRECTION??**

---

**Gen Goldman** <GENX1999@gmail.com>

to Ava

This is like that, but much fewer people care. Alex has officially quit the *Beacon* after Kent failed to replace Charlotte. Kent did promise that Charlotte would be gone by next semester, but that wasn't good enough. So Alex went rogue and posted an exposé about institutionalized transphobia perpetuated by the falsely liberal queer community. He posted it on his Tumblr, and then DigBoston picked it up for their blog. (Dig is one of the best alt weeklies. One of the first places to syndicate Dan Savage's column.)

Kent, my editor, went postal. Which for Kent means slightly mad and disappointed. He sent out an email to all the writers apologizing for the "situation" and urging everyone to speak to the managing team before going on record about Alex's resignation.

He then asked me to meet him for coffee. I thought I

might be guilty by association since Kent is apparently keeping vigilant track of all of my sexual encounters, but he just wanted my opinion. Apparently Kent is the most upset because he feels he has let one of his writers down. He wanted my thoughts on the situation and any advice I have for handling the future repercussions. Should he fight to get Charlotte off the paper or let it go? Should he apologize to Alex IRL or let him be?

It sort of felt like a parent asking me for help. Which shouldn't be THAT surprising since my actual parents are completely useless, but I always thought Kent was competent and assured. Turns out he's a scared little fuck-up like the rest of us!

I told him to apologize to Alex over email and continue the crusade to get rid of Charlotte. I have no idea if this is the right advice, but it felt like the most PC, social justice option. He nodded 15 times in a row—I counted—and then asked if I thought my hot chocolate was too watered down. (Apparently he got it once and it tasted like nothing.) I know that I'm bi/gay/unlabeled now, but I think if I was a simple straight girl with no sex drive I would marry Kent. And buy him new shirts.

I'm on my way to Alex's now. He hasn't answered my calls so I'm gonna go leave a note at his apartment. It feels romantic and old school. I hope one day we can enter a long-term, polyamorous relationship together.

*"I've got 99 problems but a basic bitch ain't one."*—G

5:32 PM PST

Why are you going to his house if he's not returning your calls?

Romance.

What does the note say???

Congratulations on your story. Here is a nude Polaroid.

You included a nude Polaroid???

Why else would you leave a note IRL?

Is your face in it???

No. Just the back of my head. Boys love that.

Is that a joke?? Because I clearly have no idea what boys like.

Awwww, babe.

They like faces.

Noted.

## GIRL, INTERRUPTED

---

**Ava Helmer** <AVA.HELMER@gmail.com>

to Gen

It's official! Everyone in my life wants me to be catatonic! I'm already on meds, but Dr. Baker thinks we should try something new. She wants me to change psychiatrists and try one of the few SSRIs I haven't already been on. I wonder what joys this change will bring me! Facial sweating? Extra weight? Unbearable sleepiness? Maybe the side effect will be something new and different! Like night terrors! The possibilities are endless when the medical community is committed to "fixing" you!

Can I tell you the scariest part? I want to be catatonic. If we can figure out some prescription cocktail that takes away my anxiety and obsessive thoughts, sign me up! Even if I have to be asleep the whole time. I am completely exhausted by the prospect of being me for the rest of my life.

Dr. Baker was strangely more concerned by my dropping out of the sorority than the scratching. She's worried that I am isolating myself on purpose so I can reject other people before they have the chance to reject me. Interesting theory, Sheri! What am I supposed to do now? Desperately hold on to people who can't stand me? I tried that all through middle school, and Leslie Jenkins officially moved.

She thinks I should make more of an effort to befriend people. Apparently I have a "standoffish vibe." It personally worried me to hear a professional use the term "vibe," but I guess there are larger issues at hand. I'm not standoffish. I've just been told to "cool it" my entire life. I'm sorry if I've somehow become too cool. (Cool in the rude sense, not in the cool sense.)

Guess that social skills class really didn't pay off!

I'm meeting with her favorite psychiatrist next week and have instructions to reach out to one person every day. I asked if you counted. She said no.

Wish me luck. I hope to be unresponsive by Christmas.

## Re: GIRL, INTERRUPTED

---

**Gen Goldman** <GENX1999@gmail.com>

to Ava

This Baker lady gets it! I told you to reach out to people! Everyone wants more friends! If just for the extra likes.

I'm sorry about the meds. But maybe you won't be on MORE meds but just DIFFERENT meds? It can't hurt to try if what's happening now isn't working. May I just suggest marijuana one final time? I've heard Xanax fucks with your liver.

In Boston news, Alex responded to my nude with an LOL. Not sure how to take that! But you know I love a good mystery.

Charlotte wants to talk about the whole thing. I'm trying to put that off . . . which is hard because of class and the *Beacon.* Good thing I learned how to sneak out of my house at 11!

**12:27 PM PST**

Going to lunch with some kids from screenwriting.

Even though I don't like sushi.

Atta girl!

Sophia's not here. I have no buffer.

Buffers dull the senses. Dive in, baby!

Ugh. I hate sushi.

Just get rice.

And put some fish on it.

## GROUNDBREAKING DISCOVERY RATTLES BOYLSTON STREET

---

**Gen Goldman** <GENX1999@gmail.com>

to Ava

While diligently studying for Earth Science: Natural Disasters, I had an epiphany. While it wasn't specifically linked to the Bhola cyclone of 1970, I like to think it was inspired by the tumultuous winds of change.

As you may remember, I have chosen to remain unlabeled regarding my sexuality (and voting party, but that's more due to an independent spirit). My high school experience was primarily focused on heterosexual encounters with an odd gay make out sprinkled in. Since arriving at college, my energy has been more female driven, with an odd cis or trans man making an appearance. What does all of this mean on the roller coaster of sexuality? Who am I? Who was I? Who do I want to be?

QUEER!

Once a slur, many in our community have reclaimed the term as a catchall for nonheterosexuality. It is as inclusive as it is vague. It allows me to engage in relationships with any possible person without having to redefine myself.

The queer community is vast and beautiful. It is a world that already feels safe yet is begging to be explored. I see no point in excluding anyone from the rich experience that is Gen.

After years of silently grappling with my identity, I feel a sense of overwhelming calm.

I'm home, babyyyyyyyyy!

G

**7:32 AM PST**

Who did you hook up with in high school????

Please only list girls. I don't have all day.

You don't know them.

STOP LYING TO ME.

I can't out people.

FUCK YOU AND YOUR GASLIGHTING.

hahahaha

If you can guess correctly, I will tell you.

Liza Perez.

No.

Casey Winter.

You only get the one guess!

You're a terrible person and a worse friend!

Congrats on being queer, you bitch.

♥👍

**PLEASE SUBSCRIBE**

**Ava Helmer** <AVA.HELMER@gmail.com>

to Gen

Curtis is a bad influence. After the final note session, he convinced me to make a YouTube channel so I could release the video. I had confided in him that I didn't think the short was good enough to submit to festivals. Instead of getting upset or offended, he shrugged and told me to upload it. There is no point in making something if no one is going to see it. I replied, "Even if it's really bad?" He agreed that *some* stuff should stay on the editing room floor, but our short isn't one of them.

So I made a channel. It's called Ava Help-her Films. The cover photo is a honey badger. I'm going to look into some channel art if anyone watches this stupid thing.

I feel very scared but also like whatever. How much worse could all of this get? Maybe a lot worse! Who knows!

Anyway, it's up there. Mostly so you'll stop asking me to watch it. After this you will probably not want to watch anything of mine ever again!

P.S. Is Help-her funny or dumb??

P.P.S. I guess it's too late now.

## Re: PLEASE SUBSCRIBE

---

**Gen Goldman** <GENX1999@gmail.com>

to Ava

HOLY SHIT! I loved it!! I mean I hated looking at Jake's stupid face, but other than that I thought it was adorable and charming! (As is the honey badger cover photo. I would maybe keep it???) I'm so proud of you, my little depressive!

I hope you don't mind, but I shared it a few places. (All the places.) My goal is for it to go viral so you can support my Cherry Cola habit on AdSense.

So great! Do another one but with just ladies! Men don't need any more screen time!

**1:14 PM EST**

I'm being confronted.

By the cruel reality of mortality?

Basically. Charlotte is forcing me to have lunch with her.

No! Run!

It's too late! She already paid.

I always knew your cheapness would be your downfall.

cash.me/genevievegoldman

**MYSTIQUE**

---

**Gen Goldman** <GENX1999@gmail.com>

to Ava

She might not be a blue shape-shifter, but oh man, is Charlotte hard to pin down. Over the course of one lunch I hated her. Respected her. Feared her. And wanted to sleep with her. Sometimes those feelings overlapped. She offered no apologies for Alex's departure and instead urged me to remain objective in my journalism. She feels as though her career has been stalled due to op-eds and personal essays she's written in the past. The best journalist remains neutral and nonaffiliated, and she thinks I have the potential to be one of the best. (Turns out my aversion to the 2-party system is favorable for my career.)

She didn't mention Alex directly once. I wanted to bring it up but didn't know how. It also felt wrong to discuss him with Charlotte. I knew he wouldn't want me to.

Not sure how to feel about the whole thing, but maybe there is nothing to feel. The staff spot is basically mine now, and Charlotte will be gone by then. I think I should just focus on courting Alex, writing, and not failing Earth Science: Natural Disasters.

Did you know that the 1972 Iran Blizzard was the deadliest of all time? The '70s were not a good time for planet Earth.

## Re: MYSTIQUE

---

**Ava Helmer** <AVA.HELMER@gmail.com>

to Gen

I don't really see a world in which you remain objective. You have too many opinions to never write an op-ed. Everything you've written for the *Beacon* has a clear agenda, and it's still your first semester. This woman is clearly manipulating you. I will personally pay for your lunch so this never happens again.

In lighter news, my short has over 2,000 views???? How did you do this?

There are a LOT of negative comments, but I'm trying not to read them.

Curtis is stoked.

**2:47 PM EST**

Want to know a little secret?

I put it on Reddit.

Oh! Smart!

How many other secrets are you keeping from me?

I'll tell you IRL.

Are you coming home???

Nope!

**5:32 PM PST**

Can I just wear regular clothes to a Halloween party and then when people ask me what I am, I reply "Basic"?

HA!

No.

What if I buy fake Uggs?

Get a real costume.

Costumes give me anxiety.

Dress up as anxiety!

How???

Giant pill bottle???

I'm just gonna wear cat ears.

**9:17 PM EST**

I have too many costumes. I'm gonna have to do a change.

What are you going as??

Pretty much all the female superheroes.

In both universes?

Don't pretend like you know.

Have fun as Iron Woman!

THIS IS MY CHRISTMAS.

## DOUBLE, DOUBLE, BOYS AND TROUBLE

**Ava Helmer** <AVA.HELMER@gmail.com>
to Gen

Well, that was a night for the history books. If the books run out of actually important things to write about.

Here are the ledes. I made out with someone last night. BUT I could have made out with two people. Now back to our story:

First of all, I feel like I deserve some recognition for attending a Halloween party. It encompasses two of my greatest fears: 1) costumes and 2) parties.

I finally found a costume after pleading with Sophia to help me. We decided to go as Republicans. I went as "financially conservative" (tennis skirt, fake pearls). Sophia went as "socially conservative" (camo shorts, fake gun). The bit worked great when we were together, but alone I just looked like a tennis player.

We went to this senior screenwriter's party. He invited everyone in the program. I thought it would just be the leftover writers who didn't have anywhere else to go, but it turned out to be a hot spot for all film students. I even saw a few Starkies, who are never spotted in the wild (MFA producers).

My social anxiety spiked when we arrived. Despite the blasting music (mash-ups of horror movie sound tracks), I still expected a smaller group. But once we got inside, it was so packed I could barely move. Luckily for me, Sophia is an aggressive partygoer who elbowed her way to the drink table in under a minute. Despite the obvious hygiene and safety problems of drinking a bloody punch, I took part in this obscene debauchery.

We ran into a few other kids from our class, who are much more fun when they are wasted. One guy, Marc, brought his engineering roommate, Shane, who was cute but short. Shane kept talking to me though and reacted as though he had never heard a woman make a joke before. Not in a condescending way. He was completely delighted. As though I was a juggling monkey. I had some more punch.

By midnight, I was sitting on a disgusting couch with Shane, who was dressed as Zach Galifianakis from *The Hangover* despite it being 2017 and no longer relevant. I was a bit drunk but still able to register Shane's very nervous hand on my leg. I was contemplating leaning in for a smooch because life is meaningless when I heard my name.

You guessed it! chinatownjake! Dressed as Donald Trump. He immediately pegged me as a "financially conservative Republican," but I quickly figured out he had already talked to Sophia. Shane stood up to shake his hand, which was nice but also pointed out their height difference. I tried to blow him off, but he asked if we could "talk."

How do you say no to talking without seeming like a huge bitch? Seriously. Please let me know for future situations. Shane rejoined his roommate, and I went outside with the guy who took my virginity and tried to kiss another girl in my childhood home.

Jake said he wanted to talk about the short. He's been getting a lot of good feedback and thinks we should do another. But this time maybe write it together. Why do we need to write it together?? Because he misses me. And boys talk in a very specific way. I tried to leave at this point, but he pulled me back. I thought he was going to kiss me, but instead he asked if we could be friends. He wants me as his friend even if the physical part of the relationship didn't work out. WHAT? I was too drunk to unpack this, so instead I slurred, "We were never friends," and went to find Shane.

What you're thinking now, dear reader, is that you have been misled. Jake didn't want to make out with me. So how could I have led with the possibility of making out with two people? Well, on the way back inside, this really wasted guy shouted, "Kiss me," and, I said "No thank you." I then found Shane and made out with him against a wall thinking about Jake the whole time. Is this adulthood? Wanting what you don't have?

Shane was a perfect gentleman the rest of the night and walked me home. But I don't want to see him again. He is too short and too earnest.

On a scale of 1 to definitely, how much do I deserve my unhappiness?

HOW WAS YOUR NIGHT? I saw at least five costumes on Instagram! Black Widow was my favorite. Great wig.

**12:43 PM PST**

Did you get eaten by a werewolf???

**1:32 PM PST**

Hello???

**3:07 PM PST**

Can you come back from the dead next Halloween?

Sry. Sry. With Alex.

Really??? What's happening??

Cant talk. He thinks it's rude.

## FRIENDSHIP GUIDELINES

---

**Ava Helmer** <AVA.HELMER@gmail.com>

to Gen

Dear Best Friend,

As you know from past friendship seminars, there are a few simple rules that help maintain a healthy relationship. One of those tips is a timely response. In this day and age, technology is constantly at our fingertips, and short of a Earth Science: Natural Disaster there is no believable moment when you are not on/near your phone. This guideline is especially pertinent when friends are separated by thousands of miles and a country.

Second, it is imperative to provide constant updates, especially following holidays and milestones. Third, it is also imperative to provide follow-up questions when your friend has important updates regarding holidays and milestones. (This is so obvious it should honestly remain unsaid.)

At this time, a full review of all suggestions and guidelines is not deemed needed, but consider yourself on probation. We here at Friendship Industries look forward to seeing improvement and hope to have a long working relationship.

All the best,
CEO, Friendship Industries

**Re: FRIENDSHIP GUIDELINES**

---

**Gen Goldman** <GENX1999@gmail.com>

to Ava

Chill out! It was 1 day.

I'm proud of you for making out with that little guy! Are you really not going see him again??? I'm not always attracted to people right away. Sometimes they have to grow on you? (No pun intended.)

Why are there no photos of your dope costume on social media? You have to get better at posting now that you're a YouTube celebrity.

BTW, have you seen this channel? You're such an Allison: JUST BETWEEN US.

**Re: FRIENDSHIP GUIDELINES**

---

**Ava Helmer** <AVA.HELMER@gmail.com>

to Gen

What the hell, Genevieve? That's it?? Did you not read any of the guidelines? What happened with you and Alex? I now require a full and detailed debriefing.

Also, I'm NOT an Allison. That girl is so uptight and her voice is annoying.

**6:45 PM PST**

Still waiting on that email.

I'm studying!!!

Oh, yeah? What have you learned?

Earth is a disaster!

## HOMEWORK

**Gen Goldman** <GENX1999@gmail.com>

to Ava

You have officially become homework. I know relationships are supposed to be work, but you're not even putting out.

Halloween was great. Jazmin wanted to go to the *Beacon* party so I made an appearance, but everyone there was getting angry drunk. I texted Alex thinking he wouldn't respond until the next day, but he told me he was at a musical theater party. I asked if he wanted me to come. He didn't reply. I took that as a yes.

About an hour later Jazmin and I rolled up to an apartment in Mission Hill. It was flooded with what I can only assume were the best costumes in all of Boston. Seriously, it looked like the Met Gala. Jazmin and I felt intimidated, but then we remembered that we are the best. Just in general.

Drunk Jazmin is a great +1 because she will talk to anyone. She was already engaged with someone who was sing-talking before I reached the front door. I knew I would have to be methodical in my search, so I roamed the hallways first. Alex seems like a guy who doesn't like wide-open spaces. By the second (and last) hallway, I had found him in deep conversation with someone I didn't even bother to register.

I thought he would be "too cool for school," but he broke out into a grin. This was the first indicator that he was heavily intoxicated. Much like Jazmin, Alex appears to be his best self when drunk. Or at least a version of himself that really likes me. Within minutes we were the ones holed up talking in the hallway. I was gently making fun of his costume (Christian Bale in *Newsies*), when he announced that he shouldn't be talking to me because I'm not a trans ally. (I know this sounds aggressive, but it was in a very flirty/forbidden fruit sort of way.) I boomeranged between defensive and apologetic for a bit until he made his second grand announcement. We will never be able to sleep together because I have lain with the enemy. I quickly replied, "I knew you wanted to sleep with me!" This made him blush, which was very rewarding.

I asked if there was anything I could do to rectify this unfortunate situation. He said no. I asked again, a few more times, closer and closer to his face. (VERY SEXY! I AM GREAT AT SEX!) He finally said he had come up with a solution. I need to quit the *Beacon.* I laughed, said "Oh, OK!" and then kissed him. The rest of the night was XXX and I would need you to hit "Over 18 to approve this content" before I send you any more details.

We then spent the entire next day together working and writing and kissing.

I'm in love. But I'm also in love with like 15 girls on Instagram I've never met so don't take it too seriously.

**2:13 PM PST**

You're going to quit the Beacon???

No. Maybe. I don't know.

I didn't say that I would.

You certainly implied it!

Does Alex know you didn't mean it?

It wasn't a serious conversation.

Anything said in an effort to get laid will not hold up in a court of law.

I think he thinks you are going to quit.

No way.

**5:17 PM EST**

Alex thinks I'm going to quit the Beacon.

Told you!!

What do I do?? I don't think he will be with me if I stay.

Oh, man. This is too sad for me to soak in the glory of me being right.

You're still soaking in it.

Just one quick .

What are you gonna do?

I don't know.

Maybe I should quit. It's not good to be associated with a bad organization.

You really think it's a "bad" organization now?

You basically went to Emerson FOR the Beacon.

I have to think about it more.

I don't think you should quit over such a minor thing that has nothing to do with you.

How does it not have to do with me?

Never mind. I'm not stepping into this LGBT minefield.

## SAME MONEY, MORE PROBLEMS

**Ava Helmer** <AVA.HELMER@gmail.com>

to Gen

Shortie got my number. Film kids have no discretion. He texted me to tell me he "had a great time" and "would love to see me again." BARF! There wasn't even an attempt at some sort of joke. Nothing makes me more uncomfortable than sincerity.

I don't know what to write back. I don't even want to write back. Why am I having such an aversion to a person being nice to me? Am I that terrible cliché of a girl who hates herself and only likes boys who are mean to her? I can't stop thinking about Jake and he TRIED TO KISS SOMEONE ELSE IN MY HOME. With my mother watching! (Basically.)

I always knew I was a mess, but I thought I had my own brand. Apparently, it's even worse than I suspected.

Maybe I should just marry this kid and get over my insecurity with exposure therapy. He seems like the kind of guy who will say, "You look beautiful," even if I'm covered in sweat and yelling about my low blood sugar.

Second option: celibacy. This is the opposite of exposure therapy regarding my deep fear of STDs, but I feel like I have already done enough self-growth for one person.

Anyway, do I have to write back????????

**4:13 PM EST**

OMG Ava. Just write back like a normal person.

And say what?? I don't want him to get the wrong impression.

Maybe you have the wrong impression.

Give him a chance.

I'm not attracted to him.

But how do you know that already?

You're going to tell me that I don't know my own sexuality????

REALLY GENEVIEVE!

You have no right to tell me who I should and shouldn't be attracted to.

hahaha

Whatever.

Write back, "Later, loser."

Not helpful.

## NATURE VS NURTURE

**Gen Goldman** <GENX1999@gmail.com>

to Ava

I hate to say this, but I might have preferred it when my dad was drinking. He left me alone and didn't send me links to books like *Radical Forgiveness.* My parents tried to FaceTime me with Hope earlier and then lost their shit when I wasn't available. They've called like a grand total of 5 times this entire semester, but I'm supposed to know when they want to talk.

I called back after Hope went to bed and got an earful about family responsibility and being a good older sister. It was my decision to "abandon" the family for a liberal arts education. The least I can do is answer their calls. What????? Do they actually believe the things that come out of their mouths? I stayed at your house for an entire week junior year and they didn't even notice!

You would think my father was the CEO of AA. He talks like he is a sobriety expert when he hasn't even been sober long enough to get an important chip. He wants me to go to Al-Anon. Presumably so more people can be talking about him at all times.

Maybe this call will hit my quota for the month and they won't care that I'm not coming home for Thanksgiving. Maybe by then he will be too drunk to realize it's Thanksgiving. (The holiday season is a real trigger.)

Just because he is suddenly ready to be a dad doesn't

mean I suddenly need a dad. I've been doing fine without one.

Poor Hope. I wish she didn't have such a stupid name.

**8:07 PM PST**

You're not coming home for Thanksgiving???

No way. Flights are $$$.

Please hold.

**8:13 PM PST**

My parents said they would cover it as an early Hanukkah gift.

AVA! That's not OK!

Why?? They want to see you too!

Who is it even a present for? Me or you?

Both??

I can't accept that.

Why? It's really not a big deal.

It's not just the money. I don't want to come home.

Wow. OK. Sorry. I thought we were BEST FRIENDS.

I want to see YOU obviously. I DON'T want to see my family.

Plus I'll be home like 3 weeks later for winter break.

I feel devastated. I had started a Gen countdown.

haha. 4 real?

Maybe.

I'm very lonely.

## CAN YOU DIG IT?

**Gen Goldman** <GENX1999@gmail.com>

to Ava

Alex is officially the most successful person I know (other than your dad). After his blog went viral on DigBoston, they asked him to come in for a meet-and-greet, and he charmed them so much he got offered an internship! It's going to start immediately even though they're already in the middle of an intern cycle. (Apparently the kids they have now aren't top-notch. Fucking Harvard.)

I talked to Kent about resigning. He freaked out and begged me not to. He basically offered me the staff position and promised that all future interim advisers would be more formally vetted. This whole controversy has really shaken him. I feel bad. He's just this straight cis guy trying to be a woke bae in a school full of queer kids. He's gotten some brutal @ replies since Alex's blog.

I told him I would think about it overnight. I really don't want to quit. Maybe I should just go straight to the source and ask Charlotte to step down. It's worth the risk, right?

I've already made plans to see her. You can't stop me.

## THAT WENT WELL

---

**Gen Goldman** <GENX1999@gmail.com>

to Ava

Psyche! I've taken it from your lack of response that you didn't think much would come from my meeting with Charlotte. You were wrong. A lot came from it. Like yelling. And screaming. And my decision to officially quit the *Beacon.*

I wanted to just talk to her briefly in her office, but she insisted I come to her apartment because she had too many organic apples and wanted me to eat some of her homemade sauce? Anyway, it was delicious.

We started talking about class and Halloween. I mentioned that I was seeing Alex, romantically, to test the waters. Charlotte scoffed and said, "You've got a real type, huh?" Didn't know what that meant so she clarified by name checking Molly. I don't know how you could compare the two other than through their shared hatred of Charlotte.

I tried to explain the situation at the *Beacon* and ask if she really cared about being interim adviser since she's going to be replaced by a more experienced journalist anyway. This came out far more bitchy than I intended and lit a fire in those dark eyes of hers. (Did I mention we'd been drinking a fair amount of wine to wash down the applesauce?)

Before I knew what was happening, we were both

screaming and Charlotte accused me of being in love with her??? I accused her of not having the capacity to love. This had nothing to do with the topic at hand, but that didn't stop us from arguing about it for a good hour. I accused her of causing Molly's breakdown, and she accused me of being an enabler! WHAT ARE YOU, MY DRUNK DAD?

I know this is extra terrible, but it felt great to really yell at someone. I don't miss much from home, but, oh, man, is screaming cathartic.

I left about an hour later having failed in my mission. I no longer have any other choice. I have to quit the *Beacon*. Maybe Alex will put in a good word for me at *Dig.* That's the point of sleeping with successful people, right?

## Re: THAT WENT WELL

---

**Ava Helmer** <AVA.HELMER@gmail.com>
to Gen

Part of me knows that I shouldn't even bother writing this, but I couldn't help myself. (You don't have to read it. Writing long emails is my version of cathartic screaming.)

I don't understand why you are doing this. If the faculty adviser was a known pedophile, I would get it. Or a blatant racist. But the interim adviser has written a few articles that could be interpreted as transphobic?? Come on! It's like you're looking for a fight! Or a cause! (That has nothing to do with you.) Alex sounds great and all, but do you really think you'll even be together by next semester?

Also, do you want to be with someone who makes such outlandish demands? If some guy told me I had to quit making films in order to be with him, you would lose your mind. You are a journalist, and he is asking you to stop journaling. (I KNOW THAT'S NOT WHAT IT'S CALLED, BUT IT SOUNDED BETTER.)

Does he even want to be with you? I feel like every two days he pushes you away. This is not a judgment on you—this is a judgment on him. He honestly sounds too self-involved to be in an actual relationship. This is Alex's fight and he has already made his point. You won't be as lucky as him. No one is going to offer you an internship for quitting.

Please know I am only saying this because I love you and I have seen you work so hard this semester. (Not in classes.) I'm just asking you to think this through a little bit more. Think about the long-term repercussions. Will Charlotte even matter once you're managing editor senior year?

I love you. Don't hate me.

A

## Re: THAT WENT WELL

**Gen Goldman** <GENX1999@gmail.com>

to Ava

I probably shouldn't have read that email.

For starters, this isn't about Alex. This is about ethics and what type of journalist I want to be. Am I a gun for hire, or someone with morals and standards? Do I want to get caught in something easy and comfortable and never grow? Quitting the *Beacon* means I will HAVE to find an off-campus internship next semester instead of resting on my college-level laurels. It's way more impressive long term to have worked at a professional publication.

Also, although I'm not trans, this is not not my cause. And why is a racist worse than someone who is transphobic? I know you didn't mean to, but suggesting there is a difference is highly offensive and ignorant. I know you don't have any personal experience outside of your rich USC bubble, but we are all in this together. (And by we I mean POC and LGBTQ.) I get that you are 18 and dealing with guys who are too short for you, but please don't assume to understand anything about my life or my struggle.

This doesn't have to be a huge thing. I just wanted to vocalize my honest reaction to your honest reaction. There is nothing more to say. So let's stop talking about it.

7:21 AM PST

Seriously??? We can't ever talk about it anymore?

If I disagree with you about something I'm not allowed to say so?

Not about this stuff. No.

Fine. Looking forward to small talk about the weather.

It's getting cold here.

Good.

## MY THERAPIST SAYS

---

**Ava Helmer** <AVA.HELMER@gmail.com>

to Gen

I need to apologize. I'm sorry that I gave you unwanted advice and interfered in your life. I'm not here to tell you what to do. I'm here to listen and support you. I'm so used to everyone (mostly professionals) telling me what to do that my instinct is to mimic that behavior. (Some might call it a cycle of abuse.) I'm really sorry and I hope I would have had the realization to apologize on my own.

You are completely correct that I don't fully understand your new life. I haven't been exposed to it, and the fact that you are out there existing in a different world upsets me. You have always been the biggest part of my world and I want to remain an important part of yours. So I asked my parents to book me a flight to Boston over Thanksgiving. I want to see you and I want to "get it."

I hope you don't find this declaration of everlasting platonic love off-putting. I understand that in a different situation (maybe even in this situation), buying a ticket to surprise someone across the country might appear stalkerish. If you don't want me to come, I'll cancel, but it felt more romantic to have already purchased it before I sent this email.

If you say it's OK, maybe we can stay at a hotel for a staycation? (My parents have a lot of Starwood points.)

*"I'm much more me when I'm with you."*—Pinterest/Ava Helmer

**Re: MY THERAPIST SAYS**

---

**Gen Goldman** <GENX1999@gmail.com>

to Ava

God damn it, Ava. You make it so fucking hard to stay mad at you. Can't you be stubborn and immature like the rest of us???

I can't believe you're coming here! How nonsexually romantic! I can't wait to show you all of Boston! You're going to hate it!

I'm sad most people will be gone for the holiday, but it will still be a great time! We can watch Pay-Per-View in the hotel room and go on a Duck Tour! (I haven't been on a Duck Tour because I'm not a loser, but it seems pretty amazing!) I can't wait to do all the stupid tourist shit no one else will do with me! And then I can just blame it all on you, like, "My friend Ava is a total square!" (THE BOAT GOES QUACK! I CAN'T FUCKING WAIT!)

Thank you for being the bigger person, as always. We will have you to thank when both of our coffins are lowered into the ground at the exact same time in 2083.

LOVE AND MUSH AND SAP,
G

**2:53 PM PST**

I need to buy a winter jacket!

It's gonna be 3 days!

Borrow something of mine.

Do you even have a winter jacket??

Close enough.

Is it clean?

Close enough.

I think I'll just buy my own.

Seems dumb.

## HOMELAND SEASON ONE FINALE

---

**Ava Helmer** <AVA.HELMER@gmail.com>

to Gen

What are your thoughts on electroshock therapy and do you think I could somehow get a student discount?

Met my new physiatrist today. He has a long beard and hollow eyes. Are you allowed to self-prescribe as a doctor, because this man was too eerily calm to not be high out of his chemically balanced mind. I thought he would want the whole spiel but he said he'd already talked to Dr. Baker about my history. He asked a few questions about past medications and decided I have to try something other than an SSRI. Ever heard of clomipramine? Me neither! But I have sleepiness, drop in blood pressure when rising from a seated position, difficulty starting urination, and dry mouth to look forward to!

So now I need to come off my current meds and transition to this? I feel like my dad with his 14-compartment pill case.

What if clomipramine doesn't work and I'm left with my actual brain?? I can't have another repeat of my 6th-grade ski trip where I threatened to kill my mom. (God, I feel bad for my parents.)

It's so annoying to be a drug addict without any of the fun.

And no, I'm not going to let you try it when I'm out there.

## Re: HOMELAND SEASON ONE FINALE

**Gen Goldman** <GENX1999@gmail.com>

to Ava

I never watched *Homeland,* so I actually can't relate to this email at all.

Have you read *The Bell Jar,* though? The shock therapy there didn't seem to work.

I'm sorry you have to go through this again. Maybe fifth(?) time will be a charm? Tell me more about this bearded shrink with the hollow eyes . . . Do you think he's married? Because I have a real daddy complex I'd love to talk to him about.

9:32 PM PST

Thanks for putting the image of you hooking up with my psychiatrist in my head.

No problem!

Will do anything for a prescription pad.

I remain worried about you.

And you're the one with all the shrinks! #irony

## SHANNON PUTS BUTTER ON HER LEGS

**Gen Goldman** <GENX1999@gmail.com>

to Ava

Yep, it's official. My roommate has been stealing packets of Land O' Lakes Salted Whipped Butter and slathering her arms and legs before going to sleep at night. I have resisted telling her that you're supposed to use SHEA or COCOA butter when moisturizing your skin. It's too fucking great to watch. She thinks she's really conning the system by not having to pay for another beauty product. Even if you *can* use actual butter on your skin, I doubt this stuff even counts as "real."

The whole room smells like pancakes.

If you can't tell, I'm a bit bored since quitting the *Beacon.* Kent, my former editor, took my resignation surprisingly well in that he didn't cry. He said, "I feel like crying," a few times, but his face was stoic so it didn't seem true. He told me I'm welcome back whenever. Not to be on staff, but as a writer, which seems like a waste of time. No one is going to care that I published a few articles for a college paper. I need titles and upward mobility.

Alex started his internship at *Dig* and says everyone is even more political than at the *Beacon.* You have to kiss this person's ass to get to even talk to that person. And everyone has incredibly hip haircuts. I want to visit him, but he said no. He is so formal and proper it's hilarious.

There's no real chance of me getting an internship before

next semester so I'm thinking of starting a Tumblr. Here are my pitches for names so far:

GEN X (obvious choice)

WHAT'S IN THE WATER? (a conspiracy blog about the Charles River)

QUEER AS FRACK (an exploration of gay youth and popular sci-fi)

You're the only person voting, so choose wisely.

**10:32 AM PST**

Queer as Frack.

YES! Obviously!

Will each post be about gayness AND sci-fi, or will you alternate?

There are no rules on my blog.

OK, but you will need some rules or else it will seem like chaos.

Each post will be in a completely different font.

I support you, but I won't be able to read it.

What are you doing?

Writing.

Trying to write.

Thinking about quitting writing.

Have you left your dorm room recently?

Yes. I have class four days a week.

Call a friend.

I'm texting a friend.

Is Alex your boyfriend yet?

Hahaha

No.

Why not?

Because we haven't talked about it.

Why not?

CALL SOMEONE ELSE.

## BIG MISTAKE

**Ava Helmer** <AVA.HELMER@gmail.com>

to Gen

I want you to know before you read this that I blame you. I was perfectly happy and fine sitting in my room. Maybe I wasn't happy, but I was fine. And then you had to make me feel like a big-time loser. So I called Sophia. That's right. I called her, which was startling to both of us. After presenting as a desperate freak, she took pity on me and invited me to her dorm where some friends were hanging out playing Mario Kart.

When I got there, I was a bit surprised to see some of the other screenwriters. I thought it would just be the kids on her floor, but because it was our shared friends it felt weird that I wasn't invited in the first place. I tried to get over the sting of COMPLETE REJECTION, but I also don't know how to play Mario Kart so the night wasn't going well. At some point, Sophia asked me to hand her her phone, and just as I did a text from Jake popped up. What? Why was my ex-boyfriend texting my friend? I couldn't see what the message said because of her settings. I tried to play it cool and instead blurted, "WHY IS JAKE TEXTING YOU?" Sophia got uncomfortable and shrugged. "He wants to work on more stuff together." "I THOUGHT YOU HATED JAKE." "I don't hate him. I just didn't want to kiss him in your parents' house." "WELL, DO YOU WANT TO KISS HIM NOW?!" Please keep in mind that there were like five other people in the room at this point pretending to play Mario Kart. "I don't want to talk about this right now." "THAT MEANS THERE IS SOMETHING TO TALK ABOUT! OH, BOY!" I don't know why I said "oh, boy." Never said it before. Going to try to never say it again.

"Please stop yelling at me in my room." So now I'm the crazy one? And not this manipulator who is sleeping with my boyfriend? I got up and walked out, expecting her to follow me so we could talk in the hall, but she didn't come. I texted her, "Can we talk in the hall?" She wrote back, "It's my turn to play." I cried on the walk home.

In case you were keeping track, I am now officially down to one real friend, Emma, who is basically too busy to actually be friends. Seriously reconsidering my parents' offer to move home and commute. Especially once this clomipramine kicks in and my blood pressure starts dropping whenever I stand up.

**1:47 AM EST**

How do you know they're sleeping 2gether?

BECAUSE OF THE TEXTING.

Do you sleep with everyone you text with?

No. But you do!

Fair enough.

I'm sry.

You will make new friends.

How???

I don't know! By living your life and being wonderful!

What happened to Curtis? Isn't Curtis ur friend?

We mostly have a professional relationship.

Do a pivot!

I'm not socially adept enough to pull that off.

I'll give you lessons when you get here.

Why are you so obsessed with Curtis?

Seems like a cool dude.

## MIGHT FLUNK OUT OF COLLEGE

**Gen Goldman** <GENX1999@gmail.com>

to Ava

JK JK. But seriously. I do not know how people study for tests. Assign me a 20-page paper, no problem. But how does anyone survive a major based on memorization? This is why reporters have recorders. So we don't need to remember ANYTHING.

I went over to Jazmin's with the full intention of studying

but instead got sucked into a wine-based drinking game. You might be thinking, who uses wine in a drinking game? Well, the answer is super-fucking-classy people. It was very cerebral. Every time I got a question wrong I had to take a sip, which was not the most productive choice since after a few sips I got *every* question wrong. Jazmin's BF was in town and he started playing too. I like the guy. For a cis guy. Just kidding. I liked Tom. (Did you forget about Tom? I did.)

Things started really getting out of hand around 1930 when I should I have been focusing on the great 1936 North American heat wave but instead was puking my guts out. It's sort of fun to puke red wine because it looks like you're dying from tuberculosis in an old movie.

I ended up staying until 3 AM. I kept texting Alex to join, but he was busy working. I hope he doesn't care that I'm still hanging out with Jazmin. She's thought about quitting but doesn't want to disappoint her parents. (They laminate every article.) I'm still trying to get her to quit. Mwuahaha.

If I pay you money, will you participate in a *That '70s Show*–based trivia drinking game when you're here? You'll get every answer right so it's not a real risk to you anyway.

The only thing I hate about college is class.

2:23 PM PST

Did you fail your test?

It was a quiz.

And . . .

Don't know yet!

Will not report back!

🙁

## STICKS AND STONES

**Ava Helmer** <AVA.HELMER@gmail.com>

to Gen

Whoever came up with that asinine saying clearly existed before the Internet. My video resurfaced on a different subreddit about student films. People on that forum did NOT like my little attempt at a movie and took to my YouTube channel to tell me. Some of the comments didn't make any sense. Especially the ones that called me a "feminist cunt." Apparently my portrayal of the male lead was not up to MRA standards and quite a few people threatened my life???? Why would anyone threaten my life over a dumb short where literally nothing happens? If anything, I would be mad that it's boring. Not that I'm trying to subvert the patriarchy.

I can't imagine how people deal with this sort of thing when they're actually IN the video. A few assholes found my Instagram and called me an ugly kike but I blocked them. (Or I think I did. The interface is confusing.)

I hate that I care. No one who writes awful comments to strangers is a nice, normal person, but the mere fact that so many people out there hate me is upsetting. I guess that's inevitable when you create things, but it doesn't make the reality of it any easier. I would take the video down, but it has so many views! Maybe I should just ride this bad PR and make another one ASAP? JK. I am not a strong enough person to do that.

Maybe you could troll all of these guys for me? That seems like a good decision.

**1:05 AM EST**

These guys are assholes.

Maybe I deserve it. The whole concept was a bit overwrought.

Shut up! No it wasn't!

If you listen to any of this, ur an idiot.

Oh, good. Now I'm a feminist cunt and an idiot.

I want to find all their moms on FB and send screenshots.

Check your receipts!

So close.

That's not how you use it???

U r not meant for this world. 😇

## WE COULD HAVE HAD IT ALL

**Gen Goldman** <GENX1999@gmail.com>

to Ava

I feel like there could be two headlines for this article:

**CUB REPORTER WOOS BOO WITH ROMANTIC EVENING**

**YOUNG COUPLE RUINS FUTURE WITH DTR ATTEMPT**

Why do people feel the need to "talk" and "communicate?" Can't we all just go about living our best lives and eating whatever we want?

I spent the last few days planning the perfect date for Alex. He's been really busy so I wanted to maximize our time. I got us tickets to a Celtics game and snuck Bova's pastries into the stadium using a large tote bag. (This is a horrible example of using my privilege to fool security.)

We had the best time at the game. I pretended I cared. He bought us peanuts and displayed traditional masculinity. I wore a crop-top jersey. Young love at its Boston-est. We even made out on the train ride home.

Once we got back to his place, Jazmin texted me. There was a party in Brookline. Alex didn't want to go. I tried to convince him. He said I could go without him. I said I'd always rather be with him.

A long beat followed where I panicked that I had said too much. I fully expected a we-should-cool-it talk. Instead he asked me to be his girlfriend. WHAT??? TBH, I wasn't even sure Alex fully liked me. He almost never reaches out, and I have to initiate all physical activity. When I brought this up, he mumbled something about protecting himself and not wanting to put himself out there if I wasn't looking for a relationship.

Here is where things got tricky. I am looking for a relationship, but not the exact kind that he wants. When I asked for clarification of "girlfriend," he rolled his eyes and stated what he thought to be obvious: "love, commitment, monogamy." It was that last one that tripped me up. I feel totally ready to love and commit to Alex, but I don't see why we need to add monogamy on top of that. I don't think that "only sleeping with one person" means you love someone. If anything, I think it can make it harder to stay in love with that someone. Why have resentment and rules? Why not just have honesty and openness?

Alex did not take this very well and immediately closed up. He said he would think about it and I should do the same. Then we went to bed without hooking up even though neither of us was that full or drunk, which are the only acceptable excuses.

He acted like everything was fine in the morning but didn't kiss me at all. That didn't stop me from kissing him all over until he said he had to get to work. I left.

Help?

## Re: WE COULD HAVE HAD IT ALL

**Ava Helmer** <AVA.HELMER@gmail.com>

to Gen

I don't understand. You have spent this entire semester obsessing over Alex. First "hating" him and then "loving" him. But now that he wants to make it real and be with you, you say no??? How can you know that monogamy isn't for you? We're 18! We don't know anything! Our brains are basically mush that can only remember song lyrics and the occasional scent from childhood.

Do you think you are pushing him away because you actually care and actually caring is scary? I can understand that fear (I would prefer to not care at all about anything ever), but Alex seems like someone who is worth taking the risk for.

I can't even imagine what he is going through right now. To put himself out there like that and have you step on the whole premise of his happiness (two people choosing each other and only each other). Don't you think there is something magical about that? I don't have more than one best friend. Don't you think it's special that I'm your best friend and you're my best friend? It says something to other people when we talk about each other. Don't you want that in your relationship with Alex? Maybe you just need to sit on this for a second. Or try it out. A healthy relationship might surprise you.

## Re: WE COULD HAVE HAD IT ALL

**Gen Goldman** <GENX1999@gmail.com>

to Ava

I shouldn't have asked for your help on this. I appreciate you trying, but you clearly devalue my feelings and view of the world. So how could you possibly help?

How come I know nothing at 18, but you are some sort of relationship messiah? Maybe if you and Jake hadn't been monogamous, things would have worked out differently. I know that your parents have the most perfect marriage known to woman, but that lifestyle doesn't work for everyone. (Honestly, how do we even know your parents are monogamous?? They could be swingers for all we know! You did find a *Playboy* that one time.)

I asked for your help in terms of how to talk to Alex and make him feel secure even though we don't want the same things. But I will figure out what to do. Jazmin and her boyfriend are open. I'm sure she'll have some good advice.

P.S. That was not a burn about Jazmin. She just has personal experience and a different POV.

## Re: WE COULD HAVE HAD IT ALL

**Ava Helmer** <AVA.HELMER@gmail.com>

to Gen

I can't believe you brought up my dad's *Playboy.* We made a pact to never speak of it again.

(This is me deflecting. I'm trying it out to minimize the time we spend arguing.)

## FEMINISM

**Ava Helmer** <AVA.HELMER@gmail.com>

to Gen

I know that's a broad subject, but I wanted to start with a disclaimer that the following incident occurred because I support feminism and firmly believe that women should build each other up yada yada.

I cornered Sophia after class and asked if we could talk. I wanted to let her know that I wasn't mad anymore. Jake and I aren't together and I have no rights over him. I don't want a stupid guy to ruin our friendship.

But she didn't let me get any of that out. Instead she rolled her eyes, said "Fine," and walked over to a different part of the hallway. I was thinking a sit-down conversation over tea, but OK. Before I could start my apology, Sophia reamed me out. She said she felt bad that I was depressed "or whatever," but I don't have any right to take it out on her. College is too short to begin with, and she doesn't want to waste it on people who bring her down. She thought I'd be better once I got out of that bitch fest (sorority??), but apparently I've only gotten worse. She's thought about it and doesn't think we are good enough friends for her to have to put up with this. If we'd been friends for like five years or whatever, maybe she would stick it out and hope I get better, but we've only been friends for like half a semester and I've been sad for most of it. So she's gonna have to bow out. If I work my shit out and get "better Prozac or whatever," she's open to us hanging out again, but honestly she would rather wait until at least next semester. Not to be rude or anything but, you know, self-preservation. She would want me to do the same if she turned into a huge drag. I get it, right? No hard feelings?

Yes, hard feelings! Are you kidding me?! You can't stop being friends with someone because she's depressed! ESPECIALLY if you're a writer. How would you keep any of your friends? I had no idea what to say. I felt like I was in some horrible after-school special where the message was: Be a bad person?

Are people allowed to say these things??? I was trying to apologize!

I'm in shock. Is my depression really that bad? I thought I was handling it very Woody Allen, annoying, narcissistic, but funny.

I never see Sophia! I mean sometimes, but it's not like I'm calling her up once a day to debate my purpose in life and test out my suicide note. I think the scariest part of all of this is realizing that I have no concept of other people's perceptions of me. Does everyone else find me intolerable? Do YOU find me this intolerable?

If you want me to cancel my trip so I don't "bring you down," I will.

**10:43 PM EST**

What is Sophia's phone #?

Gen. No.

Fine. I'll wait until you get here to steal it from ur phone.

Just deleted it.

UGH.

I'll troll her Instagram instead.

It's private.

WHO IS THIS BITCH?

Hahaha

Do you think I'm really that bad? That she had to friend break up with me?

No way.

Are you having a tough time? Yes.

But that's when you step up and be a BETTER friend. Not STOP being friends.

I found her on Facebook.

Stop!

What about Molly?

What about her?

Didn't you stop being friends with her when she went crazy?

No. I brought her back to her room, watched her all night, and then made sure her parents took her home safely.

Oh. Right.

I hate this bitch.

She is going to die miserable and alone.

Or maybe with Jake. Which would be worse.

I'm gonna take a nap.

OK. Sleep it off. It will all seem better in the late afternoon.

## CASABLANCA

**Gen Goldman** <GENX1999@gmail.com>

to Ava

I know you refuse to watch this movie because you think it will be sad and slow, but it has one of the best good-bye scenes of all time. My story will not live up to it. Mostly because it wasn't really a good-bye so much as a "see ya l8r."

I went over to Alex's house to talk, and in the theme of being bombarded with decisions instead of having a conversation, he immediately announced that he thinks we would be better as friends. We obviously want different things, and it's probably a bad idea for two journalists to date anyway. Too much nosiness for one relationship.

I thought about fighting with him, but I knew there wasn't any point. I have no choice but to be the best, sexiest, most alluring friend this side of the equator. He will crumble in no time. I handled the whole thing maturely too, which I know is a big turn-on for him.

So now I just bide my time and have a little fun. There are plenty of rainbow fish in the sea.

**7:47 AM PST**

I'm so sorry about Alex. Are you OK?

I'm totes fine. This is temporary.

Really?

Yeah. Love is an ocean.

??

COMES IN WAVES.

Oh god.

Do you think you'll go back to the Beacon now?

?????

No way. I would have quit regardless of my personal relationship with Alex.

Really?

Yes! THEY ARE TRANSPHOBIC.

OK! Sorry.

Will you still pick me up at 3 PM tomorrow even though I am ill informed?

Pick you up how?

Oh, right. I guess I'll take a cab.

AH! Can't wait!!!

The hotel looks nice.

Are we really staying at a hotel??? My bed is big enough for 2 people.

Hilarious.

If we don't use these Starwood points, someone else will!

## FULL DISCLOSURE

**Ava Helmer** <AVA.HELMER@gmail.com>

to Gen

I'm having a panic attack about tomorrow. I have no idea what to pack and I'm worried I won't be able to find a cab and then I'll be the one idiot girl Taken in America. I'm worried I'm going to be cold. I'm worried I won't fit in. And I'm worried my parents are secretly upset that I'm missing Thanksgiving.

What if the hotel room isn't nice?? What if it doesn't have Pay-Per-View?

Mostly I'm worried that Sophia was right, and when you see me you won't want to be my friend anymore.

I guess I'm equally worried about having to stay out late and drink. Maybe we can take a lot of naps in the mediocre hotel.

What if I sleep through my alarm?? What if you don't like me anymore?? What if I forget my underwear??

I just checked. I have my underwear.

SEE YOU TOMORROW!

A

**12:13 PM EST**

Did you sleep through ur alarm?

I'm already on the plane.

What time is it there?!

Oh, right. I slept through mine.

Safe flight!! Can't wait to not like you anymore!

Do you really want that to be the last thing you say to me before I start hurtling through time and space?

Yep! It was a pretty good joke.

💩

**8:04 PM EST**

Landed!!

**8:22 PM EST**

Waiting for my bag!

Gen??

**8:35 PM EST**

I think they lost my bag! I don't know what I'm going to do!!

**8:37 PM EST**

Got my bag!

Where are you????

**8:45 PM EST**

IN A CAB EN ROUTE TO THE HOTEL.

PLEASE CONFIRM I DID NOT ARRIVE IN BOSTON ONLY TO HAVE TO IDENTIFY YOUR BODY.

**8:52 PM EST**

Hi! You landed!

What's the hotel again?

The Westin Copley Place.

Great! Should be there soon!

**9:13 PM EST**

Here! Do you want me to wait in the lobby?

No, go up!

I'll be there soon.

Room 302.

That's the best one!

**11:15 PM EST**

Where are you?? This party is crazy.

By the front.

I'm by the front! Falling asleep because of the Duck Tour.

Gen! Answer your phone!

I see you.

**11:42 PM EST**

I made it back to the room.

💪

Do you have your key?

Yeah, yeah.

I'll be back soon.

**2:37 AM EST**

Why are you not back yet???

OMW.

**3:15 AM EST**

Be there soon.

**8:51 AM EST**

Went to get coffee. Let me know if you want anything.

**7:14 PM EST**

On the plane.

If you care.

I'm not the one who left.

**WHAT THE FUCK HAPPENED?**

---

**Ava Helmer** <AVA.HELMER@gmail.com>

to Gen

I'm sitting in my room at home, hysterically crying, not fully comprehending how I got here. 24 hours ago we were best friends in Boston, and now I don't know if we're friends at all?

To be clear, I want to remain friends. Not just friends but best friends until we die living side by side in a gated community.

BUT I can't reconcile the Gen I know and love with the Gen I just saw. For starters, after not seeing you for months, we finally had less than 3 days together. You chose to spend one of those days sleeping off a hangover. Why did you have such a terrible hangover? You tell me. Seems like a really weird time to get super wasted when you know I don't like to drink.

Also seems weird to abandon a girl with anxiety problems in a new city so you could hook up with the one person everyone hates. I don't understand why we even went to a party where Charlotte might be. And I REALLY don't understand the hold she has over you. This whole time I thought maybe I wasn't getting a clear picture of who this woman was since it was all secondhand. Maybe she really is captivating and deserving of your affection, despite her misguided transphobia. NOPE! She was WORSE than I could have imagined! Every word out of her mouth dripped with condescension and half the things she said couldn't have possibly been true. (No one has ever survived on just air.)

Also, what was she wearing?? Just a bunch of scarfs pretending to be clothes?? It was 40 degrees out! Unbelievable.

Honestly, if you had just apologized on Saturday I would have forgiven you. Maybe not right away, or without a few snarky remarks about barely surviving the walk back to the hotel alone, but I wouldn't have left early.

Drunk Gen is not my Gen, and I get that.

But what I can't forgive (at least not without a lengthy apology) is your behavior that next morning. You used every insecurity I've ever shared with you against me. I'm not "not fun" because I think it's wrong for you to hook up with the ONLY person the guy you are supposedly in love with disapproves of. To suggest that you were self-sabotaging isn't absurd. It was pathetically obvious. I thought we were close enough to be honest with each other, but it seems like all you want recently is a yes-woman and it's not in my nature to do that. (I literally can't do that. It's impossible for me to lie. Especially to you.)

I have no idea how the fight escalated so quickly and I have no idea if you meant all the things that you said. I certainly hope you don't believe we're fundamentally different now because you're queer and I'm straight. That's an insane thing to say and unbelievably hurtful. Think of if the roles were reversed and I said that to you. I would be burned at the stake.

My parents keep asking me questions about what happened, but I don't want to tell them. I don't want their view of you and our friendship to be tarnished. I don't want MY view of you and our friendship to be tarnished.

I'm sorry for whatever role I played in this breakdown, but I didn't say or do anything other than what I thought would be best for you. Because I love you, and you're my best friend.

AVA

## Re: WHAT THE FUCK HAPPENED?

---

**Gen Goldman** <GENX1999@gmail.com>

to Ava

I didn't mean that we were different because of our sexualities. I just meant that we are different. People grow apart. No one marries their high school sweetheart anymore. Why wouldn't the same be true for friends?

Glad you got home safe.

## Re: WHAT THE FUCK HAPPENED?

---

**Ava Helmer** <AVA.HELMER@gmail.com>

to Gen

That wasn't exactly the apology I was hoping for. I'm not even sure if that counts as an apology. Seems more like a technical clarification?

Please apologize soon so we can make up and I can tell you about how Kent, your former editor, flirted with me at the party. You were right. His shirts are too small. Possibly washing delicates in hot water.

**8:12 PM PST**

No follow-up on Kent??? Really?

We kissed while you were with Charlotte!

Naked!

OK. None of that was true, but he did friend me on FB.

I get it. You don't want to talk until you've written a beautiful apology that I will print out and frame.

I look forward to reading it.

♥

**1:32 AM EST**

Hey. I'm sorry I haven't written back, but I don't really have anything left to say. Ur still my friend and I care about u, but this is too much right now. It's taken me a long time to figure out who I am and what I want, and I really don't need someone who is supposed to be on my team sitting on the side judging. I'm 18, for fuck's sake. Not everything is so dire. It's just too much to handle my life and your emotions/ expectations. I need to focus on school and writing. U should get that. Maybe we can FaceTime or something when the semester is over? I'm planning to stay here over break to apply for internships. This isn't a big deal. I just need some space. ♥

**7:52 AM PST**

Seriously?? You need space? Who says that in real life?

Gen. I think we are blowing this whole thing out of proportion.

Can we just forget the trip?

You hurt me more than I hurt you, and I'm willing to do that! Why can't you??

**11:14 AM PST**

Cool.

**REGARDING MY LACK OF FUN**

---

**Ava Helmer** <AVA.HELMER@gmail.com>

to Gen

Hello,

I have decided to disregard your request for space because I think it will be detrimental in the long term. I have seen you push away your family and I will not let you do the same to me (even though I honestly support that; they are crazy).

You probably think I am crazy too, but that's fine. My goal here is not to convince you that I am a super-chill, normal person but to remind you of the unchill, unusual person you have come to know and love.

For starters, I am not unfun (as you suggested more than once over the course of short 54 hours we spent together). I am just not traditionally shot-glass-on-my-stomach fun. But let me tell you something: staying up until 3 AM getting wasted is all well and good in college, but will any of these kids be a good time once we hit 30? Or 40? I know how to occupy all 16 waking hours of the day sober! And that is no easy feat. Games? Love them. TV marathons? The best. Witty banter for days? I'm your girl. I'm also always down for a super-fun pool day (I do have to specify pool over beach due to aversion to sand).

I'm not hip or trendy, but I like to believe I have a timeless quality. Like, mentally, I could be 18 or 63. (Oh, man, am I going to flourish at 63. It's gonna be the new 50.)

And now for a trip down memory lane because I'm not above using manipulative nostalgia to save this friendship.

The year, 2014. Our age, 14. The style, bad. It was the third day of freshman year and everyone was still trying to navigate what it meant to be at a charter school. Some kids knew each other before. Others were able to rebuild themselves from the shoes up. I was clinging to a lukewarm middle school friendship that was on the verge of going sour. You were already the coolest person in the class. Maybe not in popularity, but objectively.

We'd already talked once (the sweater incident), but I never thought you'd remember. You wore Doc Martens and purple hair. I wore my insecurity on a button-up. It wasn't meant to be.

But then the unthinkable happened. I made you laugh. I can't remember the exact joke, which is surprising given my tendency to endlessly quote myself, but I know we were in English class and I know it had something to do with Voltaire. The next day you sat next to me ON PURPOSE, and I wrote you my first of many notes. I still think of that as the bravest thing I have ever done, especially considering how atrocious my handwriting is. You wrote back using terms I didn't fully understand yet, and a classroom friendship was born.

From there it took a few weeks for our relationship to blossom outside school. The first time you came over to my house, I told my parents to play it cool, but before dinner was even over my dad was making nickels disappear and picking your card from the stack. I was mortified. You seemed genuinely amused.

You came over more. I offered to go to your place. You declined. I tried not to be too clingy. You hung out with Cheyanne Metzner for two weeks and I cried at night. Cheyanne Metzner turned out to be a Scientologist. We were reunited. By Thanksgiving everyone knew to ask me where you were because we were so inseparable. I started jokingly referring to myself as your secretary. We got in our first fight. We got over it.

I eventually go over to your house when your parents are supposed to be at work. But your dad is home and drunk so we leave. I feel terrible and ill equipped to handle any problem that doesn't originate in my chemically unbalanced brain. You laugh it off but cry later.

We spend the next four years attached at the hip. No one understands it other than us (and maybe my parents). We are best friends. So close that it doesn't even matter that you're going to school on the East Coast and I'm staying in LA. Weaker bonds wouldn't survive that, but we're not weak. We make a pact to write to each other every day (i.e., I make a pact and force you to sign it). We separate. You call a Lyft to take you to the airport. I yell at you for that. We remain closer than ever, even when you come out as queer in a very casual way.

Sure, there are ups and downs, but there have always been ups and downs. We once didn't speak for a week because I implied you might have a drinking problem because you drank. At all. Another time, I called you crying for not calling me first. (Writing this out, I can see why I might be a lot to handle.)

But none of that mattered because we were committed to each other. Everyone always talks about the effort you have to put into a romantic relationship or a marriage, but why would a friendship be any different? You are always going to be more important to me than some random boy I marry. (At least until the silver wedding anniversary.)

I know that everything is in flux right now. You've moved. You've come out. You've started and quit your dream job. Your dad is pretending to be sober. I know you hate it when I try to "therapize" you, but I think you might be in some sort of spiral and taking it out on me. (I forgot to mention you also got dumped! I forgot because you never get dumped!)

I'm not even asking you to apologize anymore. I'm just asking you to step back, look at the length and depth of our relationship, and ask yourself if you really want to throw it away because I don't like your TA.

*"Life is too short for long-term grudges."*—Ava

P.S. Elon Musk actually said that but he invented independent space travel, so we should listen to him.

## Re: REGARDING MY LACK OF FUN

---

**Gen Goldman** <GENX1999@gmail.com>

to Ava

The joke wasn't about Voltaire. It was about Camus.

## Re: REGARDING MY LACK OF FUN

---

**Ava Helmer** <AVA.HELMER@gmail.com>

to Gen

Oh, shit! You're right! Please do not disregard my entire argument due to one factual mistake.

**2:42 PM PST**

I just saw Kristen Stewart!

She was with her GF! They look happy!

Text me back within the next 30 minutes and I'll send you a blurry photo as proof!

**3:11 PM PST**

One minute remaining before you lose your chance at an exclusive photo!

**3:13 PM PST**

 OK. I'll sell it to Star instead.

## I'M ON TO YOU

**Ava Helmer** <AVA.HELMER@gmail.com>

to Gen

I've got to give you props. At first I was very confused and deeply hurt. How could my best friend in the ENTIRE WORLD be ignoring me? The world is a terrible place, but not THAT terrible. At least in America.*

But then, while out past my bedtime last night, I realized something. You aren't actually mad at me! You are just conditioning me to do better on my own! I've been too dependent on you even though you're thousands of miles away. I know I don't have to go out and meet people because I'll always have you to talk to. But now I don't have you to talk to and I need to talk! (Seriously, it feels like I have a word quota and if I don't meet it every day, words spill out of me at the cash register, which holds up the line and causes a lot of eye rolling. From the cashier.)

By 3 PM yesterday I was completely stir-crazy. I thought about going home for the weekend, but that seemed like admitting defeat. (Also, my parents had plans.)

So I called Curtis. (I know you're a fan.) I acted casual, as though it was completely normal for me to call him up and ask what he was doing on a Friday night. He was too polite to call me on anything and seamlessly invited me to a film school party. I went, completely prepared to have a terrible time.

Instead, I stayed out until 12:30 talking and laughing with people who were drunk but not so drunk they were wearing costumes or grinding to EDM. If the playlist had been '90s music it would have been the perfect party. Sophia was there, but I took the high road and smiled before ignoring her. Curtis introduced me to a bunch of his friends, and I spent a lot of the time with his girlfriend, Darcy, who PA'd my shoot and happens to be bisexual.

I had such a great time that for at least an hour I forgot that I couldn't tell you. Or that I could tell you but you might not respond.

And that's when your master plan hit me. You were only going to ignore me until I didn't need you anymore and instead just wanted you. (Yes, this language normally applies to romantic relationships, but what we have is equally important.)

Anyway, I'm here to tell you that your plan worked. I don't need you anymore. I simply want you back in my life. Not to judge. Not to lecture. Just to love.

Well played.

Ava
*The 1% in America. (See! I learn from you!)

**Re: I'M ON TO YOU**

---

**Ava Helmer** <AVA.HELMER@gmail.com>
to Gen

Really??? No response? Maybe there is some part of your master plan I haven't cracked yet. If you're waiting for me to cut my hair or something, I might need a hint.

XO

**8:57 PM PST**

Darcy just taught me how to ride a hoverboard!

I only fell twice and am barely bleeding!

Text now for a hot pic!

**9:14 PM PST**

You called my bluff.

The photo wasn't that hot.

**TO UPDATE ON YOUR LIFE**

---

**Ava Helmer** <AVA.HELMER@gmail.com>

to Gen

So it's been a few weeks now and it feels too weird to not know what you're doing so I have decided to make it up!

Overall you've been pretty busy studying for finals. (I assume this is the main reason you haven't had time to respond to all of my delightful communications.) You're getting ready to ace your Planet Earth test, and almost all of your papers are near completion. Your hair is a bit longer than normal, but it's working for you.

Jazmin is sad to leave for break, but you guys are going to throw one heck of a holiday bash before she heads out. (It turns out that Jazmin loves Christmas, which is surprising but oddly enjoyable.)

Alex has been playing hard to get, but you've taken a page out of my book and are refusing to take no for an answer. He's going to miss you over New Years, and then the two of you will reunite in some open form of relationship next semester. It's going to be beautiful and magical, and I promise to instantly like any photo you post on Instagram.

Familywise, your parents are giving you a hard time for not coming home, but not enough of a hard time to buy a ticket for you or come to visit. Your dad is still sober but annoying, although you've had a few private moments with your mom that haven't been completely intolerable.

Hope looks adorable over FaceTime playing dreidel. It would have been wholesome if someone didn't know the backstory.

Finally, you miss me. You think about me constantly and wonder what you could possibly say after all this time. Do you need to apologize? Do you need to yell? I just want to let you know I would be happy with a "Hey." Just give me a "Hey," and I'll take it from there.

A

P.S. Can't wait for us to make up so I can see how much of this I got right.

**4:17 PM PST**

Just got home for break.

My parents want to go get ice cream in December.

You must miss LA a little, right?

**9:23 AM PST**

I keep thinking I'm going to hear from you on Christmas but then I remember we're Jewish.

**SUP?**

---

**Gen Goldman** <GENX1999@gmail.com>

to Ava

Hi. Hey. Hello.

I'm sorry I haven't been responding. It's mostly because I haven't been reading. I was so pissed when you left I tried to block the whole experience (and you) from my head. Is that classic avoidance? Yes. Did large festive alcohol consumption help? Absolutely.

I know that it seemed like we were fighting about Charlotte, but I don't actually give a shit about Charlotte. If anything, I got angry that morning because I was embarrassed. It's hard enough living with my own questionable decisions without some pillar of morality reflecting back at me. (You're the pillar, if that was not clear. And you're quite shiny.)

I almost ran after you that day, but then I started thinking about why I was so mad. You've judged my "bad behavior" numerous times in the past, and it never made me feel like ripping off the top of the Empire State Building. So something else was obviously going on. And after a few weeks of stuffing my brain with final papers and excessive scarf purchases, the answer floated to the front of my mind, even as I was screaming, "Leave me alone!"

Basically, I have no idea what I'm doing. I've been out and proud for less time than St. Vincent and Cara

Delevingne were together. It's easy to accept the queer community, but I still don't know if they accept me. So it's hard when I feel like I have to be your official ambassador for all things gay, when I still don't know how to get to the town square without using my navigation.

Is this all your fault? No. But you demand a certain clarity to things that I can't provide right now. Am I in love with Alex? Am I gay or bi? What does it mean when I kiss my friend for fun at a party? I do not have all the answers to these questions and I don't know if I ever will.

Which is fine. I'm happy to live in the gray. The gray is my home nestled between my dysfunctional family and chaotic social life. But you, Ava, like black and white. And I felt bad that I kept disappointing you.

So I pulled away. And I fought the instinct to tell you about Shannon's latest beef broth obsession. Or send you a picture of a student sleeping on a bench next to a squirrel, who was also sleeping. (So f-ing adorable. I saved it. Don't worry.)

Pulling away was petty and mean and I'm sorry. But part of this whole "self-exploration" is realizing that I AM petty and mean. Not all the time, but enough to end up downstairs if downstairs is actually hell.

That doesn't mean that I don't want to be your friend. I just want to be able to tell you about something without having to give it meaning. I want to explore parts of myself that are inconsistent or ugly. I don't want to be black and white, but I do want to be better. To you.

But I need you to be better to me too.

Gen

P.S. Wow. That was the gayest thing I have ever written.

## Re: SUP?

---

**Ava Helmer** <AVA.HELMER@gmail.com>

to Gen

My dearest Genevieve,

I apologize for not replying IMMEDIATELY as I am prone to do, but I wanted to take my time so as not to further botch the most important relationship of my entire life.

(After seven failed attempts at a response, my father dragged me to get fro-yo so I'm typing this from my phone like a cool/hip young exec who has to work weekends.)

I am so sorry. I completely disregarded how huge this semester has been for you. You came out in such a blasé way, I stupidly thought it didn't even affect you. Like you woke up and were like, "I'm queer," and then you got breakfast. Which was dumb because you never eat breakfast.

You are so brave and so strong that sometimes I forget someone like me can hurt you.

But you need to remember that you can hurt me too. I know I joke about being desperate and lonely and it feels like you can do anything to me and I will still be there, but I don't want that to be true. I don't want to be the kind of friend you can ignore or push away when you feel like it. You need to be present in this friendship if—

**2:12 PM PST**

What flavor did you get?

??????

Looks like peanut butter with rainbow sprinkles.

Are we FaceTiming by accident?

Look behind you.

OH MY GOD YOU'RE HERE.

Stop texting and hug me!

## PLEASE CONFIRM RECEIPT OF THIS MESSAGE

---

**Ava Helmer** <AVA.HELMER@gmail.com>

to Gen

Dear Best Friend,

It is with an EXTREMELY heavy heart that I say good-bye once again. Unlike the first time, however, I no longer feel the need to lay out the ground rules for what I now know will be a lifetime of friendship. Call me when you can. Text me often. And think of me constantly.

You have grown into a beautiful woman, and I can't wait to watch the rest of your transformation.

A

## Re: PLEASE CONFIRM RECEIPT OF THIS MESSAGE

**Gen Goldman** <GENX1999@gmail.com>

to Ava

R U serious??? WE ARE IN THE SAME ROOM.

U R beautiful 2.

# EPILOGUE

11:14 AM PST

On the plane!

Wahoo! Buckle up!

Thank you for driving me.

Duh! Are you gonna take a cab back?

Nah. I think Alex is gonna pick me up in his dad's car.

TELL ME EVERYTHING.

We're just friends.

Sure. I saw those texts. He's in love with you.

Sorry. No more questions.

Do you want me to give Kent a for you?

It was 16 FB messages! It meant nothing!

When are you going to upload the video?

Curtis said he'd be done with the edit by the time we're back next week.

You're gonna be a star!

Yeah, right. The Internet is gonna hate me.

Maybe. But I love you.

Love U 2.

Let me know when you land.

Always.

## ACKNOWLEDGMENTS

**Joint**

Thank you to our manager/really good friend, Matt Sadeghian, for, well, everything. We were complete messes before you. Thank you to our agents, Sasha Raskin and Jamie Chu, who took a big chance on an underdeveloped pitch. Thank you to our editor, Sara Goodman, who understood our vision after only one phone call. We are still in shock. Thank you to Mey Rude, Tiq Milan, and Kip Reinsmith, for consulting on the book. And thank you to The Lovin Spoonful, The Lonely Island, and candy for getting us through the writing process. At our core, we are just 2 guyz having a good time.

**Gaby Dunn**

Thanks to Marc and Caryn, for letting me lampoon you all the time. You're very good sports, considering. I love you both! Thanks to Cheyanne, Meme, Grandma Lee, and the first real writer I ever knew: Aunt Michele. Thanks for doing Career Day. It had a big impact!

**Allison Raskin**

Thank you, Mom and Dad, for endlessly supporting me, laughing at my jokes, and keeping me alive. I would not be here without you. Thank you to my sister, Jocelyn, for giving me my nieces, and also for being my sister. And thank you, Sugar—you're the best emotional support animal a girl could ask for.